One is Me 3

One is Me 3

The End of the Road
Or
is this just another off-ramp?

WR Mertens

aventine press

Published by Aventine Press
55 East Emerson St.
Chula Vista Ca 91910
www.aventinepress.com

ISBN: 978-1-59330-896-4

Printed in the United States of America

The Long and Winding Road
A Unique Perspective on Finding an Off-Ramp

When I came to writing sometime ago (it seems like centuries now), I always remembered fondly, my own composition teachers from years past, very confidently telling me (through their actions of the over-usage of red pen correction) that I would not have a chance in the World of Writing.

How times have changed...

Yes, red pen correction is still around, but it is not as severe as it once was. Composition teachers have changed too, from being "super-strict" and using the "do this correctly my way or it is an E for the course", to using journals and encouraging free range thinking of thoughts that were once – "never-allowed", to creativity almost knowing no boundaries.

I have been extremely proud to have been and will always continue to be a writer/author of books/educator...and I thank my composition teachers from college for instilling this process within me.

No...this is not a SPOILER-ALERT.

This is a clarification to all of you as readers of One is Me, One is Me-2 and One is Me-3. Over the years since I had published my first book (before One is Me), I have always enjoyed reading reviews of my works of published thoughts.

I have always left it up to the reader to make their own decisions, on what and how I have had my characters express those thoughts through the various settings and conundrums that they may have been involved in.

It was through the sage advice of the divine Laura Riggs, who once told me, not to stop writing and she expressed those thoughts so eloquently to me, every morning for almost thirteen years, from behind her desk. Sadly, she retired and I did survive on, for a few years thereafter (although not happily ever-after), until it was my time to go.

I hold no grudge, nor grievance against anyone at the time of my departure. It was (and still is) my wish that those in the public sector, would listen to all people and be as fair as possible with all circumstances and not to just hide behind "transparency" (that new millennial buzz-word), but are still to this day, "out to save their behinds at everyone else's expense) in the public sector.

How those persons rose to the top is absolutely amazing to phathom and on the other hand, so amazingly unintelligent. (Yes, I did say that!)

Sadly…we have come into an age, where we can say what we want, but if anyone takes offense, we have adopted a "hell-be-you" attitude, as you could be fired, censured or (worse, as I found out(even bullied out of a job. But with those experiences, it makes for a very challenging and yet creative environment in which to bring characterization to the next level.

Many people ask, "Why are you not on Facebook?" It's simple…go on Facebook and see how many phony pages there are and quite possibly with your own name attached to many of them. It is amazing to see that you said and/or did something that you did not have any part of that should explain my absence from social media.

Also, while I am a fan of social media, having been hurt by it (through no fault of my own) opened a doorway to workplace public opinion that worked only to worsen an already bad situation. My wife (yes wife!) of 28 years plus and the only woman in my life, keeps me abreast of what is going on.

Having moved on in my life in the private sector, I felt it was time to chronicle some of the misfortune with characterization through my books. They are tempered with humor, sometimes fiendishly wicked situations and sometimes – very sad ones.

The private sector has given me a renewed sense of pride in my work and in my writing, having many colleagues in many departments who have offered great insight into publishing (especially those in the third floor English office) and writing.

A great friend of many years, guru Mandy Assi always offered me a great pathway to Hindu philosophy and that through this philosophy comes great creativity and understanding in both life and the consciousness of being.

I pass this on to the readers. Don't be so quick to judge any author, writer, playwright, employer, employee, educator or friend. Read One is Me-3 (or read One is Me and One is Me-2) to see what has changed, who changed it...and why?

Stay open-minded...

THE HIGHWAY

ONE IS ME
(with apologizes to the Walrus)

"The time has come," this man has said, "to talk of many things" ---

"Of life – and death – and the going's on – of stupidity and kind".

"And why the bell tolls late – and whether tardiness is great, and the notions that pigs can really fly --- but no one still knows why?"

"But wait a bit," this man has said, "before we have our chat"---

"For some of us are out of breath and some of us have gone deaf".

"Coffee and breakfast," the man said, "is what I really need" ---

A sausage muffin with egg, besides, is very good indeed."

"Now if your ready to proceed, I know I can begin with speed,"

"But not with me", the man did cry, while turning a little blue, "after years sixteen, such kindness that would be – "a dismal thing to do!"

"But the day is fine, " the man did say," Did you really admire the view?"

"It was so kind of you to come"

"And beginning – you are very nice --- and without thinking twice!"

The Spirit said nothing but , "just cut to the chase and slice".

"I wish you were not quite so deaf – that I have to ask you twice."

"It seems ashamed that after all this time", the man did say, "to be played on such a trick" ---

"after" --- "been brought out so far --- and then to have to run so quick."

The Spirit said nothing but, "It's enough to make you sick."

"I weep for you", the Spirit said, " I deeply sympathize" -- "with sobs and tears," he sorted out --- those things of important size.

"O Man, said the Spirit, " You've had a pleasant run."

"And shall I be driving home again?", the man did say, but the answer came --- there --- none.

"And thus, was scarcely odd, because, I remained but one.

...One is Me

Madame Penelope (aka Penelope Sheinham)

Sees all, hears all and does all

We all start with other goals of what we want to be in life when it comes to careers. This includes what we currently are in life.

At the college's annual faculty-staff "Welcome Back" banquet at the beginning of the fall semester, I was surprised (if not flabbergasted) to see someone who was a "temporary" adjunct instructor in the colleges' continuing education department sitting across from me, Penelope (or Penny as she liked to be called by her girlfriends) Sheinham.

Penny had sacheted in off the street one afternoon, as if out of nowhere and managed to score an interview with the Assistant Dean of the department. The current scuttlebutt among the rest of the department was that they were looking for an "evening division supervisor" for the evening classes, which happened to include our department, of course.

She had only taught in the classroom for less than six weeks. I had also heard that she may have held an undergraduate degree with a major in marketing Avon products to third world countries. If you looked close enough at her, she appeared to have enough pancake and rouge on her face than a fully done-up corpse at a mortuary.

With the formalities of the banquet in progress, the college's President announced a list of all new staff and to which department they belonged. Having taught in my department for the past 17 years, I was thunderstruck to hear this woman's name mentioned and then to find out that this woman was now my "evening supervisor", but also put in charge of most of us who had taught in the evenings. Something told me, not to take my eyes off this woman. Obviously, there was more to this woman than meets the eye. You know when you have that nagging thought that just picks at your mind – right?

She proceeded to get up from her table, where all the other departmental secretaries, assistants, clerks and typists were seated. Now the interesting part was, Penny, as well as everyone at the table, was dressed in black – totally in black. I could understand the formality of "basic black" at certain occasions, but this was totally black from top to bottom, including their shoes, which were all standard pointed wing-tips with long black spiked heels. The sight was very eerie and on that ceramic floor, all you could hear was the "klickity-klack, klickity-klack," as those shoes moved back and forth across that stone cold tile floor.

The following night, I arrived early to go to my mailbox to get my requisite class lists and my contract, when I walked through the office and was stopped abruptly by Penny at the front desk, very questioningly prodding about "What did I want?," not "What did I need?," – nor asking nicely either. I said, "I always come early to get my things". She responded very tersely, "From now on, since I'm in charge – you will wait until I check the computer to see if your class is running or not", which I already knew it was, but I just smiled politely and nodded.

This went on every semester thereafter until I finally grew sick and tired of the nasty treatment and confronted her. I was then, very sternly reminded that "I am your supervisor and if there are any problems with that concept, we can go see Dean Freemantle and you can explain it to him", she shrieked in a very bullying tone. Well, nobody wants to approach Dean Freemantle because of his steamroller approach that he has, when speaking to people and rolling right over them.

Later that same evening, I came back to the office after having graded mid-term papers and heard strange music and noises coming from the office conference room. As I drew closer, there was an eerie blue glow emanating from the room through the crack in the door. I looked inside....

There was Penny and one of the department assistants moving rhythmically around the conference room table in what appeared to be erotic undulations, systemically moaning and groaning as though they felt some type of inner libation amongst themselves. Penny had a small pot of contained earth (which I had always seen on her desk) which she placed on the conference room table. She was wearing a long black cape, in addition to her requisite black outfit that she was always seen in. She spouted some chanting and groaning and more rhythmical writhing until she started mentioning faculty names and invoking names of trolls and ghouls and things that walked in the night.

The moon is bright, the crone is cold
The body lifeless – the bones so old
We all live and pay our dues
To die in ones and threes and twos

Death – dance and play the harp
Piercing silence in the dark
The woman's old and withered limbs
Death beckons her to dance with him

As she accepts the Dance of Death
The earth is cooled by ghostly breath
To lie in dormancy once more
To have her strength and life restored

She then, waved her hands, drawing a pentagram in the air above the table. She then invoked the spirit world again flapping her arms in the air like a bat from Count Dracula's castle belfry...

All ye spirits who walk this night
Hearken! Hearken to my call!
I bid you in our circle join!
Enter! Enter! One and all!

Oh might of the summer hands
Guardian of the dead
We pour forth sleep on those you keep
Within your urnly stead

Those who were cursed have walked these halls
That soon we shall rove
We offer curses
Curses from the arms below.

Then waving her bat winged cape around again, a pentagram was again appearing boldly in her undulating movements.

Blessings to thee, Oh Spirits of the Halls
We beseech you for your presence in our Circle
And honor you this sacred night.
We beseech you Keeper of the Sacred Dead
Damned once again those souls within your building
And those still wandering in the halls
So Must It Be!

She let out a loud shriek and she and her assistant began cackeling in delight.   Then she starts moaning in undulation to the rhythmic music as she produced a fully ripened pomegranate. She took what looked like a letter opener to the table and plunged it into the fruit, splitting it to display the seeds. She said..."*Whose seeds lie in the dormancy of death?*" Then she had her assistant eat one. The assistant cackled..."*I taste the seeds of Death!*"

She then held an apple and said..."*Behold the apple, fruit of wisdom, fruit of death...*"   She cut the apple with the letter opener saying..."*Whose symbolism rewards us with life eternal?*" She held the apple in both hands and the assistant flaps her arms like Batgirl in a pentagram shape cackling..."*Behold the five-fold star – the promise of our rebirth!*"

She took a black goblet and fills it with wine. She passes the cup to her assistant along with a slice of the apple saying..."*Taste the fruit of our rebirth and sip from the cup of life!*" which was a black chalice with gold markings. Gee, she was drinking on the job – oh my!

After she and her assistant shared libation, she instructed her assistant to name the seeds and the curses that belonged with them. They were placed in that creepy pot of dirt that she kept on her desk.

She cackled in delightful modulation again as they started to move rhythmically around the conference room table. She chanted...

This is our rebirth through the cosmic plan
In living we die – in dying we live
The circle turns ever
And I am its root!
Her assistant shrieked...
The sun conceived in darkness cold
In this death, life unfolds
A shred of light begins to burn
As the circle turns!

She stopped. She and her assistant left out the rear door and all was very quiet.

Was she trying to put curses on us poor teaching folks? Of course, she was. She was trying not to let on that she was a resident priestess of a coven that "resided" within the college's district. I thought that she was strange since taking over, but since I discovered that she was a priestess of a coven and my supervisor? This new revelation was very hard to deal with.

I should have discovered that her love for systematic undulation over the potted earth she kept sitting on that was next to her on the office counter., where I swear nothing would ever grow (well maybe with the exception of poison ivy or poison oak). These pots, I swear had cobwebs growing over them, not to mention, the spiders that crawled out of them from time to time.

She also had a mischievious streak about her. She would use her metaphysical powers to occasionally set off the sprinkler systems in some of our classrooms and sometimes setting off the fire alarms during torrential thunderstorms with zapping lightening going on.

But I digress... She was only the "head" priestess and the "High" priestess of the coven. I very quietly left out the back office door tip-toeing as not to disturb her gothic worship service, trying to put that horrid visual out of my mind. For days, all that went through my mind was Charles Gound's *Funeral March of the Merrionettes*, sadly marching over and over.

When I returned a week later though, all had seemed rather different. There were plants growing in their once cobweb infested and spider ridden pots. She was suddenly no longer wearing all black, but for one thing. Those long black spiked steel-toed wing-tipped shows were still there to remind me, was this all a dream or was she really the witch she was?

THE THINGS YOU LEARN ABOUT ANIMAL BEHAVIOR THAT YOU WOULD NEVER FIND AT THE ZOO

At some point in your life, you may have visited your local zoo. As children, we watched the lions and tigers and bears (oh my!). Little cubs and babies in the children's section of the zoo, all rolling around so friendly, in play with each other until they grow up and go to habitats more dearly suited to their now "more adult" personality types.

Human beings tend to get caught up in this evolutionary championship to mark domestic territory through the use of animal noises. The grunts, groans and even posting up signs have become a common existence. Benjamin Franklin came up with a whopper of a sign which became a short-lived flag. That motto was "DON'T TREAD ON ME" from the days of the Revolutionary War. Every time it was proclaimed, it marked new territory for the new colonies.

Now Thelma Danforth was somewhat of a new colony within herself. She started at the college as a reprographics clerk in 1987. She was paid twenty cents higher than the going minimum wage at the time and had occasionally admitted to being a wild and free-spirited thing in her pre-teen Haight-Ashbury days. However, Thelma had an unyielding zest for life, a zest that she could not quell. A fire, she had burning for her most frequent visitor to her office, Adolpho Watters, the copy machine repair man.

Thelma gave the appearance to everyone that she worked with that she was a very nice, easy going and very happily married, to the same man, with a set of twins, a boy and a girl named Aiden and Fiona. In the many "family" photos on her desk, you would see the two of them clinging to her like the day the Virgin Mary was sighted at Lourdes.

But let's go back for a moment...

During the interim period in her life, Thelma worked briefly as an Actuarial Clerk for a downtown Chicago accounting firm of WALDORF and STATLER, LLC., in some out of the way basement office in one of the many North Michigan Avenue high rise buildings built back in the day.

She kept her life to a very rigorous schedule. Everything was extremely regimented. Coffee breaks at 10:15 and 1:45 AND LUNCH AT APPROXIMATELY 12:00 Noon and not a minute earlier. You would have thought she was enlisted in some brand of the armed forces as you could set your watch by her.

One afternoon, she was reproducing some estate documents for Mr. Waldorf, when the copy machine started to sputter and clank and sound like a very old car with sawdust in its transmission. The office manager Dee-Dee (short for Deloris-Debra) called the repair man to come fix the old bugger.

An hour or so later, Thelma was surprised to see a new man on the job. Gone was her stand-by Marco, who was close to 65 years old and was with the company since the age of ditto machines. It was rumored that he liked to smell the ditto fluid. In walked this 35-40 year old man. He appeared to be very strong and appeared to have a well-defined muscle structure (in her opinion) from maybe working out continuously. His name badge said that he was

Adolpho Watters. A very strange name she thought, but she kept staring at him, gazing at his bulging, rippling muscles as he dutifully unpacked all his testing equipment and boxes of spare parts.

As she gazed at him, her computer speakers were loudly playing the Miracles song, *"I'm Just A Love Machine"* in a seductive thumping tempo just a little bit faster than her heart rate was currently running at. He looked up and spoke to her. "Hi, I'm Adolpho, but you can call me AW – most people do", he sputtered as he got to work on the machine. He had spoken his introduction with a very heavy Italian accent. She felt her knees about to buckle as she had happened to be in a very romance-less marriage at the time and really wanted more.

She sat back down at her computer, one ear to the toe-tapping Miracles song and trying to reconcile a purchase order. She waited to about the time he had finished and then left the office to go to lunch. She had the most flushed look about her face.

As I said, you could always set your watch by this woman. She got her purse and ran to the elevator and up to the mezzanine level, where she entered the *Panera* sandwich shop in the food court. She was again, a creature of habit, having walked to the counter and ordered her usual lunch which consisted of a blue-cheese crumbled salad with raspberry vinigarette. You know the type that comes in the hairspray bottles that you spray the lettuce mixture, just enough to cover, but no taste? A bottle of water with a plain bagel, cut in half and toasted with no butter completed her order. Heaven forbid! She's dieting, you know...She collected her order and walked skillfully down to the back of the restaurant where her usual table was next to the restrooms and sat down to eat.

Just then, she looked up and was about to take in her first bite of that weed-n-feed special

when a man appeared in front of her, looking for a place to sit and asked the question..."Thelma...isn't it? I'm A.W....Adolpho...we met in your reproducing room downstairs, earlier? Could I possibly share your table with you as there seems to be nothing else available?" Her eyes lit up like Christmas trees and you heard her speak with all the charm of a sex-starved high school girl panting after the football teams varsity quarterback. "Oh, honey, please sit down!", as she dropped her fork on the floor with an earth shattering jolt. She picked the fork back up and tried to remain girlish about it. "How long have you worked at STATLER and WALDORF?, he enquired with that southern European dubonette charm and Italian accent that he had going for him. She replied coitly, "Oh about 15 years or so. I was hired just after I graduated college." "Oh", he asked. "Where did you go to college?" She replied, "Thornbury Women's College in Thornbury Illinois...you know...just outside of the Quad-Cities area?

She thought that this was marvelous. Sitting next to her was someone, who was only 40 years old, attractive, but was lacking in the brains department. Seeing this as a golden opportunity to mold him the way she wanted him, she continued the conversation, although more was said through the looks that they had in each other's eyes as if Kismet were the psi-psi fly of love and they were enthusiastically bitten. Soon lunch was over and he excused himself from her company by kissing her hand like a proper European gentleman should. Then he was off and so was she. He to his truck and she to her "reproducing" room (as he called it with his terrible English pronunciation),

They continued to see each other whenever the machine needed to be repaired. She would always time the service call around lunch time, so that the two of them could "dine-together" at the Panera in parkade.

Fast forward about ten years later, STATLER and WALDORF was investigated by the Securities and Exchange Commission for felonious insider trading of stocks and other financial securities and the company ordered liquidated. Poor Thelma was out of an extremely good job. Now what was she to do?

She had been in a practically loveless marriage with her two younger children Aiden and Fiona (now in high school and college) and she didn't know where to turn. What could a now seventy-three year old woman be able to do and still keep and eye on her children? Then, an idea struck her.

Fiona had come down to her bedroom after returning late from a date one night, having been home on a weekend from college. She was quite interested in giving her the HELP WANTED section of the THORNBURY FALLS-POST, the college's newspaper. In it was a job posting for an interim teacher of business, a departmental secretary and a temporary copy clerk.

The next morning, she applied for all three positions as she was now a most desperate woman (although no more despicable than usual — for other reasons — survival). It seemed that about this time that her non-responsive husband was also forced out of the workforce and was not seeing to her needs nor keeping her in the lifestyle in which she had become accustomed too.

You see, Thelma is a "ME" person. What is it that you can do for "ME" was critical to her existence and station in life. She continued to look upon herself as the Queen and the rest of those around her as her "worker bees". She dictates and everybody does that. So much for the drones!

It seemed that her daughter had hit on something. She could be a stay-at-home or school mom and still get paid for her time.

She was called in for a panel interview of significant importance with two deans, and administrative assistant and an office manager.   This was the college's interview team from Human Resources to interview her for (of all things), the position of a temporary copy clerk. They put her through a very rigorous interview, which was nothing short of having two spotlights shining on you in a darkened room and you were being interrogated by Symbianese Liberation Army terrorists and you were their captive audience. They went on and on – for hours about her business skills and how well could she take shorthand and create a power point presentation.

On and on they went, until the interview finally concluded. She wiped the sweat off her forehead and took a deep breath, the moment she climbed back into her deep maroon colored Pontiac Vibe that she had been driving. She had no sooner drove out of the parking lot when her Blackberry rang. It was the committee. They wanted to schedule her for a second interview at 9:00 a.m. , the next morning. She said it was fine and disconnected the call.

"What am I qualified for?", she gurgled to herself as she ran through the drive thru window at the Mr. Shrimp, stuffing a Number 6 in her mouth, as she was feverously fighting the noontime traffic trying to get back to her house.

She did get the job of the "reproducing clerk" as Adolph called it. She had beaten out a buxum blonde from the town of Towanda, who was a bouncer in a bar in her off hours. She finally thought that she still had that "something-something" that Adolpho was seeing. The home fires were really burning on all pilot lights now. In short, she believed she was again cooking with gas.

Now it seems that with our domestic economy having tanked as it does, with all funding cut about once every ten years and has its trickle-down effect and everything then gets cut, including the main things – money, budgets and people. And so it went...

The college Board of Trustees deemed it necessary in a round of budget cuts, to close the Reprographics Room which had been attached to the college bookstore since the last century. It still had merchandise display cases in it. A board level memorandum of intent was issued to the staff stating the impending first round of cuts in the budget and the probable consolidation of the old reprographics room with the college's current print shop.

This angered Thelma and it meant the eventual removal of her office and her job and at the age of 73, who would hire her? Now during the course of the school year, the college President appeared to have other plans in mind. He had devised a way for all staff and faculty to submit items to be copied "on-line" directly through the internet link to the print shop, by-passing reprographics, but still showing the Board of Trustees, that they were observing the current "green" trend of not using (nor wasting as the case may be) tons of unneeded paper. She thought to herself..."Whatever happened to taking good old-fashioned notes!...Now, it's a free download...What... Save a tree?" She did not like this new arrangement. But let's back up...

Thelma's marriage was on the skids, but when was it not? This lady preferred to work for years at minimum wage, plus twenty cents rather than get a "real office job". But who said that Thelma didn't play the field? Every time one of her machines would either explode, drop its transmission or would just otherwise sound like an old fashioned train wreck, she would call Adolpho.

Adolpho had a service route with the college since about the time Thelma was still employed at STALER and WALDORF back in the McCarthy Era. He knew how to keep his clients occupied and busy for weeks (even days on end). She had learned from him at his "paper tray one".

The copy machine through a horrific fit, not even on her first day out as the new clerk and she had to call for service. When the repair person arrived, she was sitting at the computer by the wall, listening to her internet radio connection playing the FIREBALLS song, "You are the woman that I always dreamed of, I knew it from the start", when Adolpho entered the room.

Their eyes met. She ran to the counter. He mouthed, "Thelma, is it you?" She knew, she had found that he had again had that certain something. Many times and over many visits, he would come in after she had placed that "oh, so special" service call, and then you could watch their eyes meet. If you remember the Muppets "Miss Piggy" and her infatuation with her "Kermy" (aka Kermit the Frog), you would understand her basic animal desire to dominate the world as she knew it. And so, she began her relentless hunt for her Adolpho. This was her very own version of Occupy Chicago.

The copy room would be very quiet in the extreme early mornings at the college. One morning, I had to come in early to run several quizzes and tests that I had to administer to my classes later on in the day. Our department secretary (not Ms. Seinham) had always kept a spare key for use by the adjunct faculty, who kept odd hours because of classroom schedules. I found the key and proceeded down the corridor towards the door of the copy room.

As I grew closer, I heard strange noises coming from the direction immediately in front of the in the hallway. I drew closer towards the door itself. I heard the most beastly moaning and groaning and the computer was playing the song, "I'm just a love machine" with the speakers volume turned up full blast.

The next thing I heard was a primal yell like Tarzan in the Sarangetti and the door of the back closet come crashing down and there was Thelma – beating her chest and wearing leopard body suit and sprawled on top of her Adolpho, whose clothes were in shreds.

You talk about a she-beast! She was beating out her native drums on top of Adolpho. I decided not to enter the den of the primal beast within, for fear that Thelma would force her inhibitions on me as well.   I quickly re-locked the door and returned the key, forever having that visual burned into my retina's forever.

"...And to think this was started by a Mouse that roared" (apologizes to W. Disney).   Above her desk, still attached to the wall was a stitched sampler that reads..."ALL MACHINES DOWN – YOU MUST SUBMIT".....but to who?

AND KEVIN HITS NUMBER THREE...

Now Maybelline Simmons was an intense woman, about 52ish in age. She too, had appeared as if out of nowhere, much like Kevin's last wife, who disappeared in to the abyss some time ago, with her renegade bandit trucker. While I must admit to not knowing much about this lady, it was said that she mysteriously appeared at a St. Louis Cardinals baseball game at Busch Stadium on a beautiful sunny afternoon.

Kevin was on a three-day layover from a delivery to a Mercedes-Benz dealership in the greater St. Louis area. He walked into the ballpark and immediately went to the concession stand where he bought popcorn, soda and enough hot dogs and pizza slices to endure as many extra innings as he could stand for his mutual replenishment.

He sat in the stands in the sweltering Midwestern summer heat, when his eyes became transfixed on this very intense woman from across the third base line. Now this woman must have been lying across third base from the look he had on his face. You didn't think all that drool was just from his ravenous appetite and the plethora of hot dogs, dripping in St. Louis-style trimmings, did you?

As the game continued, it was as though their eyes were intertwined on each other. Out of the blue, he woke up, out of that almost hypnotic trance to find her sitting next to him in the bleachers. "Buy me a hot dog?", she whispered in his ear. The next thing you see is that he was off like a flash, running to the concession stand to get the lady her "hot dog". You would have assumed that she had already found one with the way in which he ran out of there so fast.

He came back only minutes later, out of breath and looking like he was about to pass out from a technecardia. "Oh, Honey-Baby-Thanks," she whispered in his ear. He sat down and tried to regain his oxygen loss. But he still could not take his eyes off this woman. If this woman were a car, she would be described as having the largest overhead luggage compartment imaginable, but with too much junk in the trunk. It helped to her advantage that her luggage rack was exceeding the capacity of the tank top she was wearing that day.

She sat and ate the hot dog as the game went on and on into extra innings, then without any hesitation, she whispered in his ear, "Your place or mine?" He explained that he was just visiting St Louis and she answered, "Oh, that's good..let's go to your hotel room", and they were off without a care in the world. And so began Kevins folly down life's path – the third time.

Several days later, he arrives back at his neighborhood and began to pack his clothes and other personal effects and told his mother that he was moving into a new home. A house, he said that he was renting on a month to month basis. This new neighborhood was in the far south suburban area around Westerfield, Illinois. Westerfield held a special spot for him since this was where he and Maybelline were going to live.

Now how is this guy going to pay the rent, the utilities, car insurance, etc.? He figured that it was time that he used his insurance settlement from a horrible accident that he had suffered in the workplace, which left him powerless , in the automatic power windows and brakes department. Only a permanent prescription for Valvoline kept his chaisse functional (or at least as functional as Maybelline liked it).

Then came move-in day. Kevin and Maybelline and all their stuff.

Now Maybelline's only vice, next to drinking, was that she chained smoked like an oil refinery, on top of being an asthmatic. Gee, you would think that something would have had to give...wouldn't you?

On a recent trip to the hospital, she very nearly did herself in. Her not-yet husband liked to keep her in automobiles (at least ones that ran), so she could keep going to work. Work? This was a new concept for most of the women in his life, other than walking around intersections aimlessly late at night or looking for security positions to guard Slurpy machines. Those that only want things given to them for their own benefit...but let's continue...

She had another asthma attack recently and with the sorted amount of cars that she utterly had blown the engines out of, while eluding police chases on the I-762 corridor near where they lived, Kevin had decided that enough was enough and decided this. His thinking was...well.. "If your going to kill yourself smoking, your most certainly going to kill yourself from eluding the police and since I'm sick and tired of buying you new cars, guess what your next car is going to me?

The day came when she was about to be released from her hospital stay and she called Kevin to come get her. He said "fine." He walked into the hospital as the nurse was wheeling her chair to the front door of the building. The nurse-attendant said, "You can bring your car around now." He replied, "Sure honey, I'll be back in a second."

The next thing you see is Kevin, pulling up to the door in front of her in an old black hearse, complete with the curtains and space for the "cargo". She took one look at it and screamed, "Oh, hell to the no!" He got out, opened the "cargo" door and said "get in!"

They did eventually go home, though not together. He, in the "go-go" wagon and she in a taxi cab. They still don't discuss that day ever....but they did marry and you can find their lives prominently displayed through the avenues of social media.

On another of Kevin's premarital departures to was to visit him at his new residence at the Pink Cloud Motel on route 6 in Rochelle, Illinois.

You wonder how this came came about?

After his split with his first and second wives, Kevin was in a sense - homeless. Even his own mother refused to take him back. This was how he ended up at this glistening pink motel with the full length mirrors adorning the room ceilings.

She knocked on room 1312 very softly and Kevin opened it looking rather startled. She said, "What's the matter, baby?" She noticed immediately that he was most upset and all of a sudden he started to cry, because of the terrible fight that he had with his mother. His mother had paid dearly for his mistakes (his past two wives) and wasn't going to take anymore of his issues. She had officially disowned him. He took it quite badly at first.

He busted into a river of tears upon seeing Mabelline and she was quite taken back by seeing

Kevin's softer side.   "What's the matter, baby/",
she asked as she snuggled him to her bosom.   He
choked back the tears to blurt out that his mother
had just disowned him and he was living at motel
permanently. He cried himself to sleep.

She tucked him under the covers and kissed him
on the forehead and said "Good night baby?".
He said , "Goodnight Mom".   She thought "what a
momma's boy" but she liked him as she headed out
the door and left the motel parking lot.

Then finally came the day that they got married
- like all of Kevin's previous weddings, they were
courtroom affairs.   Having been to two of his past
hitchings, I said that I would pass on the third.

Now fast forward to about a year later and the
now new Mrs Kevin feels that she needs a cruise.
During the time leading up to this cruise, she held
a very decent job (other than bothering rush hour
traffic) at a hospital.   Yes, she got herself hired at a
hospital, but what's wrong with that?

If it were you or I...nothing.   If it were Maybelline, it
was a totally different story.

You see that Maybelline wants this job so bad
that she used her "friends" network to get her in. She
passed the multiple interviews and took dozens of tests
and shots for virtually everything that soldiers would
probably catch in the armed forces in Afghanistan.

Finally the start date for the new job is the middle
of January and the temperatures here are 70 degrees
below zero with a 90% wind chill blowing at 40 miles
per hour. Did I mention that she and Kevin had moved
out of state and she would need to commute to the
job. This entailed a railroad commute and getting
up at 5:00 a.m. for an 8:00 start time, not to mention

the 50 minute connecting bus ride and elevated train transfer to the job site.

Quite a lot of money spent just in commuting alone not to mention the hassle if you drove it yourself. Oh, but she loved this job for about a month or so into it. Then she claimed to have sprained her ankle falling over her janitorial bucket.

But what luck! She fell at a hospital! They will see to my needs! Right...wrong....they did she to her sprained ankle, but in the initial diagnosis for the workmen's compensation clainm, she discovered that the doctor of record had listed her as an "Unusually large" woman and also recommended weight loss to help "speed healing"

When she found this out, she tried "the doctor's way of losing a few pounds - watching what she ate. This lasted all but a New York minute. She ended up going into the hospital employee break rooms after various celebrations and ate whatever leftovers she could get her hands on.

Her subsequent doctor visits for workman's compensation revealed that she had put on even more weight and this just got the doctor very upset and the doctor would not release her to go back to work until the poundage came off.

So what was Maybelline to do?

She could not afford to live on the one third salary that workman's compensation gives you while your recouperating. Then she had a brain storm.

One of her internet site girlfriends suggested a weight loss clinic. She thought to herself.."a weight loss clinic? Yeah right.."I'm really going to lose all this weight in a hurry?

She drove herself to the "clinic" located in a store front area of a busy city intersection. After yelling various obscenities at traffic as she parallel parked her car at the curb, she got out and entered the building. This clinic specialized in liquid "herbal" supplements that guaranteed that you would go from a size five to a size negative one in three weeks, by only ingesting these moldy green shakes, which looked like something the Linda Blair character in the The Exoricist movie had thrown up during a holy water sizzle with the priest.

She thought that this would be great, three weeks to a more manageable her. She had bought into their sales plan, hook – line – and sinker. Oh, did I mention that they were also a medical marawana dispensary as well? That would tend to cast a lot of doubt on the "greenness" of her weight loss drinks, especially how "euphoric" that you felt, immediately after you had consumed one, or two or three, as the advisor had read to her off of a card script.

She went home and anxiously began her regiment of the slippery green goo.

First day out, she hated the stuff – the taste. "That stuff could take the paint off the side of my car", she complained.

Her next try was to mix the mix with two cups of granulated sugar, remembering and old saying that her grandmother said about it taking " a spoon full of sugar helps the medicine go down."

After she did this, she enjoyed the shakes or did the shakes enjoy her?

The next three weeks, she spent sitting on the toilet, not feeling well at all after each one of her shakes, but she enjoyed drinking them with all that sugar.

Now came the next problem, with these "cleansings" of her weight, but ingesting all that raw sugar for the three week period, she got the "shakes" and the "trots" and upon the next follow-up visit to the doctor, she was now diagnosed as diabetic and the doctor complained at her all the more about the weight loss. She was "livv-ed"

She was finally able to be released to return to work a week after the next doctors visit.

She returned to the job only to be followed by the doctor constantly reminding her about her weight. She lusted in her heart for bags of Oreo cookies and it was in her visits to the employee break rooms, that temptation called her name and she was back eating at the communal calorie through again.

This job was history for her after about three months. She complained to Kevin that she was being harassed by the doctor and that the endless commuting was too expensive.

No way...she just wanted to sit and figure out which way life was going to take her.

But with the exception of the weight loss shakes regiment, she kept on with those. Even with the excessive sugar intake and her other problems of COPD, she soldiered on. She spent time in retail at a local Walmart store, only to be told what to do by a supervisor and she was history in about three weeks. As she quoted herself many times, "I'm outta here!"

Poor Kevin.

During the cruise, all she did was drink herself under the Captains table. Otis Campbell had nothing on her. She also liked to go walking on the beach after going on a binder. On one instance, she was halled into jail for being drunk and disorderly and Kevin had to bail her out of the drunk tank.

Maybelline and Kevin are still together, oddly enough and this vicious cycle just continues.

But, you know what?

Maybe the third time, might be all the charm that Kevin needs to make this one a "home-run".

To those who live virtually and vicariously...enjoy.

VIEW FROM THE PEW AND LIFE TOO

Many times on Sunday mornings, I would be sitting in the University chapel prior to services, trying to contemplate, my busy (sometimes too busy) life and let myself slow down and reflect on things.

The great thing about the University Chapel is that almost every Sunday, they have a guest preacher give the homily. The messages that they impart to the congregation were three-fold; Social Action, Enlightenment in Life and Salvations Pathways.

Rather than my explaining each of these, I will let each homilist tell you, their thoughts as they preached to this very diverse and sleeping group over the span of three Sunday mornings. The FIRST is by a minister from India...this one is subtitled "Jesus and the Buddha". The SECOND is by a priest from a Spiritual Enlightenment center in the Mount Airy community --- this one is subtitled "Justification and the Path to Life". "The THIRD and final homily was from an attorney, who had been involved with social justice, both in his own community and in his own church ---this one is subtitled "Social Justice".

FIRST
"Oneness with Yourself and God – Jesus and the Buddha"

The birth of Jesus begins with his incarnation, having been born in a manger of very simple means, in a very simple setting and of human parents. The Prophet Buddha, on the other hand, had a different birth route. *He was born into a royal setting, with rich parents.*

True, Jesus was a descendant or a relative to the royal house of Kind David and God, however Buddha was born directly to his royal heritage as a Prince, son of a Kind and Queen. The parentage of jesus is reflected of both his earthly parents and his heavenly Father.

Angels foretold the shepherds in the fields that the Good news had arrived on earth that Jesus the Savior of the World (or Messiah, if you will) coming had happened and that he would be found in the form of a babe in simple means, in a manger, where they paid homage to both Him and his parents.

Buddha's revelation that he was to be a Savior of India and of the world came only after his birth, when his father, the Kind called his priests and scribes to predict his future and that his path in life would be that of a King and Conqueror, but not as an heir to this kingdom, but to the Kingdom of truth. Buddha's path was that he was to grow to be a true person or truthful to himself, answerable only to himself.

Now, eight days later, according to Mosaic law, Jesus was presented at the temple by his parents to Simeon, an upright and holy man of his time, for whom it was foretold that, he would not see his death and achieve his goal to be with God in heaven until he saw the Lord's Messiah.

Joseph and Mary presented him at the temple to serve Simeon and to do what was customary for him much like that of Hinduism's stage of life or that of student learning while still providing service to a master, gaining knowledge through serving Simeon in the Temple. Simeon's explanation of having the truth foretold and then revealed personally to him is recorded in the Biblical Canticle, the Nunc Dimittis or Simeon's Song..."Lord, let your servant depart in peace, my eyes have seen your salvation". This song of seeing God's salvation revealed to him and to all who were to come into contact with this Jesus, the child.

With Buddha's life, he had the Kings own goals imposed on him with his own hopes that he would someday succeed him as King, rather than go out into the world and not discover the true meaning of the cycle of life, birth, old age, and death and eventually gain the knowledge and understanding he needed to comprehend it all.

Now Mary and Joseph wondered about what Simeon had said about Jesus that he was destined to be a sign which all rejected and that they too, would be disappointed and hurt as parents because he would eventually disobey his parents and get separated from them at the festival, to only be found by them, gaining additional knowledge from the teachers in the temple.

Buddha's life is similar in the fact that he too, disobeyed his father and went out to see all the sufferings of the world or what it was really all about, for which his father had ordered him not to see to gain the knowledge of why these things were happening as a part of life in general.

Jesus parents wanted him to know why he was treating them like this by disobeying them, but he answered that why did they not use common sense and know that he was in his Heavenly Father's (God's) house (the Temple), where he first acknowledges to his earthly parents that he is acknowledging them as well as a higher authority of being true to his other Father.

As Buddha saw for himself that there was sickness , old age and death, and so to Jesus saw this with Simeon (who was blind, probably from disease of advancement of old age) finally advancing on to his eternal rest with God. Finally, growing up, both Buddha and Jesus grew in wisdom and gained knowledge and favor with both God and their inner beings.

Now Jesus and the Buddha had a lot in common in the ways, they handled the subject of human temptations, but also they had slightly different approaches in handling the problems that Mara or the Devil proposed to each of them.

Buddhas' first temptation took the form of desire, where Mara danced three goddesses in front of him to get him to disrupt his concentration. He probably thought he (Mara) could appeal to Buddha's human response of desire or craving for beautiful things to get him to submit to his actions. Buddha handled this temptation by continuing to meditate and not break his concentration through his practice of the Nobel Eight-Fold Way, specifically that of right speech, effort and mindfulness, not giving Mara anything substantial in which to base on argue and reason.

Jesus first temptation was similar with that same form of human desire where the Devil used the example of asking him to use his extraordinary talents given to him by God to turn regular stones into ordinary bread to satisfy the human desire of hunger, for Jesus had been fasting for nearly forty days.

Because he was fasting, this probably was a very strong desire, but when posed with this request, he answered the Devil contrary to Buddha's ignoring Mara, telling him that it was written in the scriptures that there are other things more important than bread.

Instead of practicing, the way of right speech and not speaking to the Devil, he posed to the Devil, the fact that, it was more important to Jesus to remain in this state of consciousness to possibly achieve his path to Nirvana and not go against his Father by using his talents for other than what they were intended for or that of right intention to renounce the Devil and that right view is to respect God.

Buddha's second temptation was that of the form of terror when Mara sends down armies of demons to attack young Siddhartha with weapons, great storms and rains to destroy his concentration and meditation to achieve his oneness with nature, handled this much the same way, he handled the first temptation, again following the way of right speech, effort and mindfulness and again not giving into Mara's wish and temptation.

He was probably expressing subconsciously that he was already one with nature and why should the terrible side of nature be such a bad thing, when storms and rains help to promote beautiful skies afterwards and the rains watering the earth to promote growth and newness of life.

Jesus second temptation of the Devil wanting to give him all the kingdoms of the world, if he were to bow down and pay homage to him, shows Jesus reaction to the Devils request as following the way to right action, right intention and right effort. Jesus already knew that many kingdoms of the world were already his or that of his Father's, so why should be accept the Devils offer. He responds to the Devil's request that we must worship God (his father) and Him alone as it is written in the Christian scriptures. The Devil, clearly was not intending to give him anything, only that he wanted him to renounce his Father and acknowledge him as a higher power and was not using the right effort to get Jesus to give into his request.

Buddha's third and last temptation was than of Mara's questioning the right of Buddha to be trying to achieve what he is doing and finding his path to Nirvana by reason. Buddha, here again used the path of right concentration, having sought by way of meditation, a chance again to find his inner self.

But Mara still wanted him to give into his temptation, but Buddha breaks his silence of right speech to inform Mara that he may not understand all that he was doing, but others might or one could say he was being true to himself.

Jesus third temptation was that of temptation by reason as well. Jesus was taken to the roof of the Temple and told by the Devil, "If you are the Son of God", to jump off the roof and let the angels catch him and not let harm come to him.

The path which Jesus took to address the Devils temptation was that of right intention. He responded to the Devil by telling him, not to put the Lord God to foolish test, apparently telling him straight out, if you are to tempt me with foolishness by reason, you are also tempting his Father (God) and so he was appealing to a higher power or as with Buddha – a higher level of consciousness.

If you want to compare these two paths, another name we could use would be the Lost and the Wasteful.

The parables of the Lost Son and the parable of the Prodigal Son are both very similar in their intentions that what was lost, being a Son, in the case of the Prodigal, and the poor man in the case of the Wasteful, who was in reality, the rich man's son who was found again after realizing the different paths that they each had taken to find their goals in life.

The differences appear in the story of the Lost Son that the Rich man did not acknowledge this poor man to be a son (probably because of a past indiscretion) but did want him to prove himself worthy of being a son by doing work for him and only then did he find him worthy of being a son and proceeded to leave him all of his vast wealth as an expression of love and affection for him. The son had lived a very poor life versus the son in the Prodigal story, who already received his money and spent it on fast living.

In the story of the Prodigal Son, the story that Jesus tells of two sons, one who asks his father for his inheritance ahead of time (where as the last son did not get his until later) and goes out and squanders his wealth on wine, women and fast living. The other son, choosing instead to stay home and live and work for his father and collect his reward later upon his death, questions his father's motives, when the father spares no expense in welcoming back the wasteful son and not show the same affection towards him, offers much the same explanation, to him as the father in the Buddha story, telling him that his brother had to prove to himself (unlike the brother in the other story) that his way of life was going to lead to ruin and he would eventually have to return home to continue his existence in life and also that he did not stop loving his lost son, just because he had left and no differently than he did the son still at home. His love was equal to both sons and his father's love was equal to his, so much that, of God and of Jesus, his Son.

Buddha's last instruction shows that he was to find lasting peace with himself through purging himself of absolutely everything – cravings, desire, thoughts, moods and seeing inside himself, his fullness or oneness of being and attaining Nirvana. This is something relative to purging of your sins (secret thoughts, desires, craving, moods, etc.) either publicly or privately to a priest, the acknowledging of doing a sinful act or having a sinful being and feeling better, when you purge yourself and tell someone. This is an expression of universal love for yourself and others which could be a possible vehicle in which to obtain that very same Nirvana.

Jesus provided much the same answer in the account of the crucifixion. The bodily purging of Jesus' sins even though he remained sinless before Pilate. His address to the women in the crowd, who mourned and wept for him, that they were not to weep so much for him, but that they should weep for themselves and their children. To think of themselves , and to turn to their own sinfulness and purge themselves of their sins.

This was also shown in the crucifixion, when he was nailed to the cross, when he asks his Father to forgive the sins of those that were doing this to him. For what we are doing to him was to help him achieve salvation for all and oneness with God and to show all, whom he really was, in his inner being.

The criminals who were crucified with him provided insight into this. The first criminal who taunted him, telling him to "save yourself and us", was rebuked by the second criminal who knew and saw through the outer being of Jesus and knew he had not committed any wrong, but yet he was there for a purpose, repented and asked forgiveness of his sins and to be taken with him into the next life.

Finally, realizing that his work to achieve what was to be done was finished, he committed his entire being to God and died, achieving his oneness with his Father. Amen.

SECOND
"When you walk past your alley, what do you see? The Inate oneness of Injustice."

The prophet Amos writes that no crime or injustice towards anyone or anything should go unpunished according to the word of the Lord.

You see crime and injustice, just about everywhere, even here in our own country and for me, in my own back yard.

Having lived in the greater Cincinnati Ohio area for about four years, no crime so much, although there was some, but the injustice of hunger in Cincinnati was to a great extent a big problem for most everybody residing within a four county radius surrounding the Cincinnati Metro area.

We were eating dinner at a local Friendly restaurant in the suburb of Milford, at a table positioned with a view directly across the street adjacient to a loading dock and dumpster of a local Kroger supermarket. It was almost dark. Twilight. Just dark enough where you could barely see what was going on.

In the faint light, we could see an old broken down, rusty car drove up with its lights off. Then, a family of four persons, two children and their parents got out of that same car and watched as the Father helped his two children into the dumpster behind the store and the children began handing back to their parents, cans of food, loaves of bread and bruised vegetables and produce that had been discarded by the store as waste, which they hurriedly put into a big box and placed it into the rear of their car and drove off just as quickly and mysteriously as they had appeared.

It really does make you think about those less fortunate in the area and surrounding neighborhoods, especially if you, yourself, should happen to be somewhat better off than the persons who were sighted in the dumpster, especially while one is eating dinner in a nice restaurant and for us, even now with the Thanksgiving holiday, not far off.

Although, that is but one picture of social injustice dealing with our recessionary time and hunger in the world, it brings to mind a scripture passage from Isaiah 55 vs. one to three..."Say there! Is anyone thirsty? Come and drink – even if you have no money. Come, take your choice of wine and milk, it's all free! Why spend your money on food stuffs that don't give you strength? Why pay for groceries that don't do you any good? Listen and I'll tell you where to get good food that fattens up your soul..."

And the passage goes on to remember the terms of God's covenant with David. For those without substance should turn to the Lord for strength, not against him.

Hunger continues to be both a problem and an injustice to many. Our churches social ministries committee was formed to help deal with this problem and many others that exist today in the areas of poverty and hunger with the economy in a constant state of recession and the many companies that continuously downsize and let many people go., often for no real-substantial reason.

In a closer context to help deal with problem of hunger and social problems in our society, our community dealt with this problem in a variety of ways

One way to approach this problem was to include it as a point of study within the seventh and eighth grade confirmation classes on human suffering and injustice in society. As part of the curriculum, the class members were required to go once a month as a group to the Over-the Rhine section of downtown Cincinnati to serve an evening meal at a local soup kitchen to the poor and needy.

It makes for some very humbling experiences, when you see young adults who would much rather be hanging out at McDonalds or Burger King, suddenly stop and think about others for a change and not themselves alone.

Our committee also provided for a noon meal once a month for less fortunate children at a local day care center. The Pastor had also joined our group that day, serving food to several of the children. He later remarked in a Sunday morning homily following that "most of these children did not seen, even for one minute grateful to be receiving a hot nutritious meal, much less thankful or to even say "thank you" " to him or anyone else.

In a personal observation, I believe that he had forgotten one important thing, that of the poor and even small children (though some) hold close their dignity and are good people and not recognizing this , went off in the absolutely wrong direction, not remembering that even the early tribes of Israel were a proud people and maintained their dignity and decorum, even when they were held captive in Egypt and did not probably say "thank you" either to the Pharoah, when they left.

The Pastor, I am happy to say "woke-up" to this fact and did change his opinion of those children, when he received a "thank you" card in the mail several days later, having then realized that he had violated one of the six major themes of catholic social teaching, that life and dignity of the human person. These actions provide for social action of helping to deal with the injustice of hunger by understanding the response which it had made.

In the Aprocrophic book (or story if you wish) of Daniel, Bel, and the Snake, it recalls another great tragic figure, Daniel, who heeds God's command to destroy King Astyages Babylonian idol, that of Bel or the dragon snake.

This was a difficult and very monumental task for Daniel, much the same as God's calling of the the prophet Jeremiah to serve him, even though he had failed in many of his tasks. Difficult decisions are very hard and sometimes impossible to deal with , but we all have them and have to face these decisions no matter how difficult they may be.

Several years ago, after the death of my younger brother, I was left to the care and tending to my elderly grandmother of age 86.

She was a fully functional person until she suffered a very mild stroke which required that she be hospitalized. When it came time for her to be released, there were all kinds of problems, mostly because the hospital wanted her directly admitted into a nursing care facility, necessitating spending quite a lot of money for her daily care and food. I suggested strongly that she be able to return to her own home, where she would be guaranteed her privacy, her dignity and most of all remain in her familiar surroundings.

The hospital finally agreed only after I had submitted proof that I had scheduled round-the-clock care (nurses, nurse aides, etc.) to watch her when she came home. I provided the proof and she was discharged the following day. Meantime, there was endless decisions that needed to be made regarding her meals, her medications and most of all her finances. For someone who was only 21 years of age at the time to become the guardian of an 86 year old woman is quite a burden and you soon find that your free time and freedom are nil.

The decision to let my grandmother spend her final years at home was difficult enough, not to mention a bit ahead of its time. It was three years later that in-home healthcare private agencies began to be formed as an alternative and even cheaper form of care than sending someone to a nursing care facility that really doesn't need to be there.

I felt that home health care had an advantage of providing the things that a nursing home could not. The proper dignity and respect deserved by a person of advanced age. You have to remember that this was very pre-Obama care and dignity and respect of patient rights were respected but only to a point. Healthcare today is much like a drive-thru. Yes, you can have it. It is affordable for most, but you are still not treated with dignity and respect – only as a financial commodity.

Please remember God's rule. Treat all injustice with dignity and respect and help each other to provide service to all who are less fortunate. Shalom. Amen.

THREE
"Pathways to Existence"

Namaste

Peace to you.

Salvation to us has come, a hymn of justification by God's free grace and favor. This hymn makes note of the fact that in doing good works in this lifetime, cannot control, how one's life is going to be affected in the hereafter, but by faith in God alone. Only through this can one achieve salvation in their existence.

The Indian gurus or holy men subscribe to a salvation process which we call Yoga of for others – Meditation.

In the path of Jnana yoga – the path of knowledge, one can find a path to salvation in educating oneself through studying. A student gaining knowledge of God through contemplation of literature like the Bible and applying that knowledge to their everyday existence.

In the path of Bhatki yoga – the path of devotion, one can find the path to salvation through spirituality as part of one's life through a prayerful and peaceful coexistence in personal meditation. This is where one can devote time where one can be at peace with oneself and God forsaking all other things that are going on around them in a world and leading to a loving and spiritual coexistence with God and achieving salvation from God.

Throughout Christianity, there are several examples of paths to God through knowledge and the paths to God through loving devotion to God and to others around you.

One example of a path to God through knowledge would be that of a seminarian or postulant. This person after receiving a calling from God to a vocation in religious life to become a priest or religious. They go on to attend schooling to study the sacred scriptures as an outlet to knowing God through a better understanding of the written word of God, whereby, through taking final vows or ordination, they may apply this knowledge and insight of knowing God through their studies in dealing with parishioners in the care of ordained clergy or in daily life, prayer and in service to others, in which would be the case for a religious order (nun or brother).

A second example of a path to God through loving devotion to God and to others would follow two different examples, one of which would be St Francis of Assisi. In many prayer books, there is a prayer attributed to him, we should be instruments of peace, where we should be of devoted service to God through service to others.

In this prayer, it makes many connotations that accordingly, it is better to love, than to be loved, to serve others rather than be served, to forgive someone of an offense rather than hold a grievance (which is sometimes harder than it looks!) for ultimately when we die, having done good works by serving God as well as others, we have a better opportunity next time, to be born into eternal life with God.

Another example of the path through a loving devotion to God and others is Jesus Christ as recorded in the Bible, in the Gospel of John, chapter thirteen, verses one through seventeen or the portion of the chapter referring to Jesus Christ's loving devotion to his Father in heaven for having given him everything he needed during his earthly life, gave it back or repaid his Father by serving his disciples by washing their feet as an act of servant-hood, showing the disciples that through service to others, they may obtain their path to God through this path of blessing.

In the path of work and action, Karma yoga or finding God through work, a very practical example would be the story of a very rich man and a very poor man as told by Jesus Christ in the Bible, in the Gospel of Luke, chapter sixteen, beginning at the nineteenth verse, concluding at the thirty-first verse.

The story of the rich man in hell begins with a very important and probably, a very professional man, very rich, making a lot of money from his job or investments or whatever, living very well for his means. On the other side of this story, there is a very poor man . A man who is probably on welfare and working a minimum wage job and leading a very minimal existence.

The poor man would come to the door of the rich man asking for some kind of charity. The rich man who prospered in his joy of work and luxury , turned him away and asked him to leave, not providing the man with any help or kindness. The poor man, who also had taken great pride in minimal work and his earthly existence, soon died and his soul was carried off by the angels to be with Abraham and to enjoy the many benefits of Heaven.

The rich man also died and his soul was taken to hell where he was eternally tormented for his lack of service to God and devoting of himself to God through his work and not achieving any inner peace.

The moral here – the poor man had followed this path through his minimal work and existence on earth and was greeted with a better life and existence in the hereafter.

My own path to God would be through work or Karma yoga. As a Christian, I can say that I am able to best serve God through my everyday existence through work, both at home and in the schools, by studying and learning. By recognizing that most all faiths and religions are basically the same, having a mutual respect for God, known by many names and having many of the same paths to salvation in everyday existence.

Namaste. Amen.

Chip City Blue –
Before the boats came sailing in...

Many summers ago, we took several summer vacations to the region in southwestern Ohio, called greater Cincinnati. The city of Cincinnati was home to many diversified companies, most notably, Proctor and Gamble. Its other nickname was Blue Chip City for other obvious reasons.

It was also the home to its famous two and three and four way chili dishes, ribs and quite a bit more. But the most famous things that Cincinnati is known for, are not advertised, yet still well known by the locals in that area. It was their use of the word "please and the presence of loons.

When we first traveled to Cincinnati (and it seems like decades now), we made the trip by passenger train, disembarking at the Cincinnati train station. It was a very small, very upscale, type of modern rail depot, which said, on the sign attached to the building, "CINCINNATI, OH". Unknown to us, it was actually located north of the city, about fifteen minutes, in a rather, seedy looking warehouse district.

Being from the northern part of the Midwest, we half-heartedly expected, that the depot, would be located in the city, preferably, in the downtown area and rather close, or at least within walking distance to the hotel that we would be staying at.

Wrong, again! So, we walked into the depot and had the ticket agent, call us a cab. The agent, a slightly chubby man named Bob, who looked a lot like Luciano Pavorotti, called us a taxi. We took our luggage and waited out at the curb.

The cab arrived, driven by an African American gentleman named Herman.

Herman was quite a character, very knowledgeable in his profession, telling us where the various sites to see were and the places that we might want to go. He was sort of a one person, personal (yet unofficial) tour guide to Blue Chip City.

He, later, dropped us off at our hotel and we figured that was that. Not! He, sort of, became our unofficial chauffeur between what was to become our new house in the area and the train depot. So much so, that, in fact, that we were eventually given his home telephone number and told to call him directly. What service, the two of us thought! If, this kind of thing, goes on here in Cincinnati, it must be a great place to live.

Well, how nieve, we were in our thinking, because when you first think about Ohio or Cincinnati, you automatically think of things like the Cincinnati Reds baseball team, then Mayor Jerry Springer (yes, the talk show host, newscaster and other silly things) and the fictionalized television sitcom reruns of WKRP in Cincinnati.

We stayed at the various motels in the area, checking the area out thoroughly, to see if we would eventually get married and settle there. We found things to be quite a bit laid back, in such a way that they do things, but we figured that we could live with that type of thing or style of living.

Well, after many, many trips to the Blue Chip City area, we were subsequently, forced into making a decision, that was going to be changing both of our lives forever. Back in Illinois, we eventually, had to sell a forty acre parcel of land back in Sedgewick, and we were being forced to move, rather abruptly, because of a no account, good for nothing, greedy, except for one million, two hundred thousand dollars, worth of money we received, from this residential land developer, that we sold the property to, wanted us off the property and the land within forty-eight hours after the real estate closing took place in Sedgewick.

That left us with quite a dilemma on our hands, as it seemed that we needed a house and we needed it fast and since, we really did like (or so we thought) the greater Miami Valley area, we contacted our attorney, to see if we could stall the developer and greedy group of renown purchasers, to look in the Cincinnati area for a house.

We looked and happened to drive into the Tanglewood subdivision, just outside of Milford. Nice name – Tanglewood. For those of you, who really want to find this town, I suggest you don't, because you could get lost, all too easily, by taking a left at the interstate highway and a right, back past the herd of goats, left past the pigs and another hard right, past the jack ass on the corner. This is the very first time that we met some of the really native, local peoples of the area, the ya'all and please crowd.

We ran across one house in the subdivision that we both could both agree upon that was built on land. Most of the homes in the area were built directly into hills or hanging off steep cliffs. We saw several of which had lower level family rooms located in the subbasement that were conveniently located about two feet from a ditch, which as you could imagine, probably floods, during the heavy rainy season. Think of the flood insurance rider!

It so happened that (as luck or fate, in this case, fate) would have it that the house we chose, was still open past the open house scheduled from one to five o'clock in the afternoon and the real estate agent was still in the house, cleaning up. We knocked on the door of 1236 Dustybreeze and a rather skinny, really odd sort of woman had come to the door. She introduced herself as Ms. Reba Park-Volz. This woman invited us in, to tour the house and show us all its features and everything else, that they can sell you, short of a bill-of-goods and the Brooklyn Bridge and the deed to Manhattan Island.

"Oh, what a wonderful house," she exclaimed, over and over and over! All the time, her children, Jake and Beulah, were somewhat, quietly playing around downstairs. "Oh, you have to see the combination hot tub, bath tub in the Master bedroom (they didn't call them suites then), it's just that kind of thing...for those very romantic nights, with a bottle of champagne and the glowing candles and bubble bath." Boy, I thought to myself, now they are resorting to using sex to sell real estate. This was after the time of the "Stepford Wives" but before the "Wives" shows in primetime became popular on television. The market must have been pretty depressed, but on the other hand, just maybe, she would give us a good price on the house.

She continued on with the sexy selling scenario, trying to appeal to my wife, to lure her thoughts to something a bit more tempting and then try and talk me into signing on the dotted line. Yes, her vocalized visual of very sexy nights with the champagne, bubble bath and candles in that small of a tub just wasn't cutting it. We went on to the other rooms of the house with the same attitude, nieve and stupid as ever, but ever mindful that we had to be out of our other house, twelve days from yesterday.

After some very intense negotiation with attorneys, we signed on the dotted line, only after our attorney informed us that Ms. Park-Volz, was also the builder of the house, or so it seemed and that she had to prove that certain liens were removed from the house. She provided proof at the closing, in the form of affidavits, stating that everything was free and clear. We signed and were now moving into our new home.

We moved parts of our belongings in several trips and eventually started meeting the various neighbors and others from the neighborhood, a veritable sea of loons and looky loos. It seems that people in the area are so caught up in themselves, that they are either richer than Onasis or are the high pressure, power broker types, the movers and shakers, the yuppy puppies, the various persons who worked for all the best companies that had offices in the area and held (at least) a position of Vice President in Charge of something. Anything lower would really be beneath their personal standing in the community.

The first in the cast of thousands of loons to land on the door step, was a neighbor lady from down the street named Mollie Wensted. She rang our doorbell as we were still unpacking the various boxes and alike. "Hi, I'm Mollie Wensted, your neighbor from down the street and I wanted to be the first to say welcome to the neighborhood." She was nice on the outside and probably on the inside too, as neighbors went. After all, we were only in the house, just two days. "I just wanted to give you this little basket of goodies. I know how things can be on moving in day," she exclaimed.

Then as quickly as she arrived and before we could invite her in to talk, she exclaimed that she had her mother in law in the van and that she was already fifteen minutes late for her doctor's appointment, and with that, she flew to her van and burned major rubber, down the driveway. How odd, we both thought, that she was the first person in this neighborhood to say hi and welcome. We thought that was a custom that died out with the dark ages and wasn't practiced in this day and age.

Not soon after, we met our new neighbors, next door, to the north of us, the Brantfords, who are a charming couple, to say the least. Over the time span of approximately two days into our new home, we did hear from them. Not in the regular, knock on the door or ring of the doorbell mind you, greeting that you would expect from a new neighborhood, but a very terse and almost bizzare letter, mailed to us.

I got the letter out of the mailbox at the end of the driveway and immediately opened it. I thought to myself, how odd, especially for neighbors of all things, to send you letters. I thought that, maybe it was a greeting card or something, but no, it was a letter. Having reached the front steps, I called for my wife to come out and see this very fine., welcome to the neighborhood, we had just received. It seems that, in addition to various other things that we didn't know about the house, we just now found out. Our builder and real estate agent, one Ms. Park-Volz had neglected to inform us that she had our driveway poured right up to the property line between us and the Brantfords.

It seems that when my brother in law drove into the driveway, he inadvertently drove slightly off the driveway on the Brantfords side and the letter was warning us ever so tersely, to not do it again, as that side of his house contains a lawn of one hundred per cent Kentucky bluegrass sod or some other species liken to it, that was "now ruined" in that spot and what did we plan on doing about it.

It went on to state that he would be at home for private consultation regarding this matter. We were both so incensed over this issue, that we personally did not speak to either of them until about a year later, after we had a landscaper fix the problem. We both apologized for the problems. He – for writing such a letter that he did and we – for causing the hole in the first place.

But, as common sense would have it, six months, after we paid to fix the problem that he was ever so gracious to bring to our attention, we caught him outside, digging a three quarter foot trench all along our driveway to 'help alleviate' the standing water problem between our yards. That was our introduction to the southwestern Ohio culture, the part where you "do as I say, but not as I do".

Again, after we were moved into the house, we did not throw up any drapes or sheets across the windows for privacy. Not just yet, as we were told by Ms Reba Park-Volz, the realtor and builder, that chapter five, subparagraph two a, in the homeowners association rules and regulations stated that we could not do that, because, it was 'not considered proper' as they rationalized it, but the way it comes across, it was simply not allowed at all. So fine!

We happened to be in the Master bedroom and heard some very loud talking outside the house. We looked out of the window and what do you suppose we saw? All four of our surrounding neighbors as bold as day, sitting with lawn chairs, gathered in the neighbor's driveway, who was located directly across the street from the master bedroom window, sitting there in the total darkness, watching and laughing themselves silly, watching us moving around in our bedroom. To them, this must have been the most fun that they had had in years, short of going to a peep show. I mean, it (at least for me) took the meaning of voyeurism to new heights! Needless to say, up went the bed sheets on just about every window and door in the house from that day on, until drapes arrived.

Over a period of time, some of the neighbors, dis start to warm up to the fact of having us for neighbors was, somewhat okay, even though, I was unemployed and that my wife, still had a job and was 'reasonably' employed, by their standards of acceptance.

The Brantford's had two sons. One, for which we never knew his name, was supposed to be in his final semester at Ohio State University. He would often appear at home on various weekends and other special occasions. We soon found out that he was getting married, through the neighborhood grapevine, and that the wedding was going to be held in a Middle Eastern country, and that the family was having a sort of pre-wedding party prior to the send-off. The evening before the party, all sorts of wild and strange things were going on. The usual things, caterers, housekeepers and furniture rental places were coming and going all day long. We left to go out to dinner that evening to return to the strangest of all events, that ever took place in that house.

We drove into the driveway and my wife suddenly stopped the car. "Hey, will you look at this," she said to me with a very confused gaze on her face. "Isn't that

Aaron, the Brantford's kid, up there?" Sure enough, there we were parked in our driveway with half of the other neighbors gathering as well, to watch the goings on. There, bold as you be, was Aaron Brantford, in the upstairs hallway bathroom, who window faced the street, stark naked, as the day he was born, dancing around the bathroom with his everything exposed to the neighborhood. The damn fool forgot to close the curtains in the bathroom and draw the shade for privacy. There he was, exposing himself to us and the neighborhood. With the kind of crowd that had gathered, one would have thought, you had a ring side seat in one of the stripper bar establishments in the Red Light district of northern Kentucky. From what we had heard, this is supposed to be the 'Bible Belt' and that this behavior is not to be tolerated. Not! It seems that even the holy people get horny too. They just don't know how to take care of it properly.

Neighbors, to know them is to like them, I guess. Except that, when you have neighbors across the street, that act towards you, like you are just utter, gutter trash. "Oh, what do you do for a living," said Mr. Klinton (no relation to the Arkansas family late of the Washington DC). "Oh, I'm self-employed. I do desktop publishing at home," I said in response to his question. Answering that question was, sort of the kiss of death to this man and his equally repulsive wife, Driscilla, as it went from that day, we first met them, after they moved in. You see, David and Driscilla were the neighborhoods very first brown nosers, apparently, having both, come from upper northeastern coast breeding and by the looks of the both of them, they acted like their ancestral lineage ran all they back to the Pilgrims and the Mayflower.

Who really knows that, perhaps they did date back that far. Their people were probably the servant class that rowed the boat.

The Good Book says to love your neighbors as you would yourself. Right? Wrong! Try as you will, even a Nun would have trouble digesting that one. You see, these two thought that they were moving into this really exclusive neighborhood. Well, that is what they thought. They were conned by the same person we were. Ms. Reba, coincidentally sold and built their house as well.

These two were unusual, in the fact that David supposedly worked for some company and worked out of his home. Driscilla, his wife, did absolutely nothing. She was a housewife, there to answer the door and do nothing more. They had three sons and two daughters and a dog. Mrs. Klinton would leave in the early mornings, sometime around eight o'clock and take the children to school. These children, her precious charges, went to the public schools and Clermont Valley High School in the area. You see, these children were so spoiled that they had to be driven to school each and every day of the school year, and just taking the big yellow school bus that stopped just right outside their house, just would not do.

After, supposedly dropping off the kids at school, she would continue onward to probably visit and perform various charity works in the general area. Meantime, five minutes after the wife, Driscilla, left the house in the morning, in pulls this car. A beater? A bomb, as it were? Call it what you will in this neighborhood. It was Mr. Klinton's secretary, a rather sexy woman in her mid-thirties and very stacked. She got out of the car and just walked right into the house, as bold, as you please, just as if she had lived there. This always led to suspicions, that these two were having quite a torrid, love affair in the daylight hours. Suspicions rising from the fact that she would always leave five minutes prior to the afternoon arrival of his wife and children, who were personally picked up and delivered home.

The other thing that was quite strange, was the UPS delivery man who made deliveries to that house, every day, at the same time and always, just let himself in the back door of the house, just like the secretary and never left for at least twenty or so minutes. Compounding this, we had a regular UPS delivery man on the street and this was not him. This type of thing is still probably going on today. A love land haven for afternoon delight of passions.

In another incident, the children had a graduation party or something like that. The guests for this party, started to arrive about four in the afternoon on Saturday. The guests just kept on arriving, carload after carload after carload of them. Not the average alcohol drinking kids, you would expect at a graduation party or other high school type party, but very well dressed kids. Suits and dresses were the order. Car full after car full of them, parked up and down the street. Dustybreeze looked like a Hollywood Premiere on Oscar night.

Then it happened. The cars were filling up one side of the street. Mercedes, Porshe, Lexus, Lincolns, BMW's and limos. Up one side of the street for three blocks to the north and and four blocks to the south. Then, up our side of the street, until they were blocking our driveway. That was the straw that broke the camel's back. The car that was blocking our driveway was not a Lexus, but a full fledged Rolls Royce Cornische, complete with, what looked like a solid gold hood ornament. My wife and I spent most of the evening watching from the window, staring at the various guests that were arriving and we both agreed that it would be in our best interest, to go over there and inform Mr. Klinton, that he would have to move the car from our driveway. My wife went over there and knocked on the door. She was mortified to find that Mr. Klinton was incensed, that she politely asked him to move the car and that he proceeded to tell her off and that she had some nerve for even asking.

She came back to tell me that, when the door opened, there was loud rock music playing and that she saw several scantily clad underage girls in thong style bathing suits, drinking alcohol and dancing erotically in front of Mr. Klinton to his mutual delight. When I asked about Mrs. Klinton's whereabouts? She told me that for all she knew she was in another part of that house entertaining. What part, I already knew.

This man, Mr. Klinton had the sense that the Almighty gave a jackass. One morning, he was leaving and proceeded to run over the dog and kill it with the back end of his car and keep right on going. Realizing, what he had done, he pulls over, gets out of the car, picks up the corpse and drops it in the garbage can behind the house. He gets back into his car and drives off. He didn't care what he had done and neither did Driscilla or his children, either, for that matter, as they all didn't think anything of it. They probably thought that it was cheaper than euthanasia at the vet.

Our other neighbors, the Dobose's, lived across the street from us on Dustybreeze. Roger and pam and their lovely yet, stuck up daughters, Hillary and Janette. Roger was a member of the highly honored, upwardly mobile, young executives group, to which, most of the other husbands in this neighborhood belonged. His occupation in life was that of a Vice President with a local hotel management firm located in the Cincinnati area. Pam, on the other hand, was a wife and to most of the rest of the neighborhood, a real airbrain. Her mentality consisted of two brain cells, one positive one negative and nothing else in between. Pam's occupation, was that of a terminally bored housewife, nothing to do all day, after sending the girls off to school, except to walk around her house in her scantily clad nighty and read cheap, taughtry romance novels and eat Laura Price bon bons, all the time. You would think that with eating, all those bon bons, this woman would have the thighs of the Pasadena Rose Bowl, but with a size two body, it never seemed to work out that way. We often thought that there was a car (other than the ones that they owned) in the driveway, it always lead everyone in the neighborhood and ourselves included, to believe that this woman led a very questionable lifestyle, between the hours of nine a.m. and four p.m., so to speak.

Roger and Pam led, what would be called in most circles as a very fast paced upwardly snobby lifestyle, only associating with the best of the area's crème de'la crème . If you had an upwardly mobile six plus figure job in the Cincinnati, it was "Oh, Hieee," and a short wave as she was passing you on the street on her way somewhere.

It was only, three months before, we even remotely hinted around that we were planning to put the house up for sale and move out of Cincinnati, that Roger and Pam decided that we were even remotely worth being considered as probationary friends, much less even offering to help me find a job in the area.

For three solid months, she dogged my wife and I, to try and get our friendship, under the guise of her recently completing her Ohio real estate licensure. She would come over and schmooze about as tactfully as a stockbroker, who wanted you to invest in tax free bond funds covering Rio Dejenario banana farms. She went so far as to, finally (after knowing the both of us for a good part of the last four years) inviting us over for dinner in her home, with her two snotty children.

That, we could have done without.

The menu for that meal consisted of the following: Breast of Turkey with Mashed Potatoes, corn, and some kind of dessert, that looked and tasted like hell.

We had both thought at the time that this was quite possibly, a sincere effort on the Dobose's part, however after we found out that we were being served a meal of Breast of Shoe Leather Turkey and Mashed Potatoes (with no gravy), horse corner and some dessert that resembled soggy cardboard from a cereal box, we soon assumed that our suspicions were correct and that we were being played for suckers. But, we both agreed that you have to give these loons, the benefit of the doubt, but as we found out after that and what was still to come, was that you can't trust people like these as far as you can throw them.

When it finally came down to wanting to sell our house in Ohio, she schmoozed so much that we finally became sick and tired of it and gave her the contact to list the house with the local realtor of Schister and Boris. Those fools, coincidentally were the same ones that offered Pam a job, after she graduated from real estate school. No sooner than we signed on the dotted line, she promised both of us, with all the tact and finesse of a person kissing the Pope's ring as a sign of obedience, that she would do everything in her power and exhaust no expense in methods of selling our home. Right? Think again!

It took her twenty five newspaper ads, three walk-throughs and one Saturday afternoon *Parade of Homes* video program taping and six months later, did she finally land someone to buy our house? No! Her house! Which she coincidentally put on the market, just across the street and did not tell us about it. And she was listed as the broker!

What a colossal, stab in the back! She sold her house and had people through her house and it sold in two months. What was she doing for us? Apparently, very little. When questioned about her supposed, underhanded tactics, she just said that it was just the "luck of the draw" and that was that.

"Oh and by the way, did I mention that Ohio law just changed and you have to sign this addendum to your contract, which allows me to be a dual sided realtor or a buyer-broker, which allows me to represent not only the buyer as well as you, the seller? " "And that just benefits everybody!" Everybody, wrong! She collects a commission from the buyer for representing them as well as from the ones that are originally selling the house. A win, win situation? For her, and not for you.

After five months of hearing nothing, we called her to find out what she was doing regarding the house.

Our phone calls were always intercepted by Roger, who would lie and tell us that she was either in bed asleep (at five o'clock in the afternoon, right!) or she could not come to the phone right now and that one of the kids was sick.

We tried again on Halloween afternoon, only to have her answer the phone and tell us that, in no uncertain terms, that we were interrupting her family time and to call back later. How rude!

We discovered one thing about the way people do business in the State of Ohio. If you are contracting with someone or something to perform a service for you and you know that you need it done right. First thing, is to get it all, spelled out in writing. Second, always make sure that the persons or companies involved are bonded and insured. And third, if you do business with anyone, always stand over those persons or company representatives, while they are doing their jobs.

This is most important, because if you don't do this, you couldn't even prove in a court of law, that the job was done to your satisfaction and you will be left with a very shotty repair or construction job.

One final thought on the subject. The burden of proof is satisfaction in the State of Ohio is the most difficult, if next to impossible thing to prove, and if you doubt the word of someone or company in this area, they will start to flap their wings and sputter and honk like the flock of loons that are always either on the decks or swimming around the river boats on the Ohio River. Watch them take flight quick.

Beware.

CAMPUS GATE

Back in the early 1980's, the third job that I ever held was when I was attending school at a local community college in Green Hills, Illinois. Like most of the students at the time, I was in need of financial assistance and accepted on-campus employment as a student worker in the Office of Campus Safety and Security (now known as the Campus Police).

This was a cushy job, that paid you a bare minimum wage and you would work very short hours with relatively little to do. But, that was the way it was. At least for the first year on the job, anyway.

Like most students, I was very happy to know that I could take comfort in knowing that, somebody in this world, was willing to employ a college freshman, with very little clerical skills.

The first person I met in Safety and Security was Jackie, who I went to see, with my application in hand for an interview, or so I thought. This was my introduction to the world of public safety and what it really didn't do for me was to begin to define the words true meaning.

I walked into the office, which at the time, was located in, what used to be a small three bedroom house. One of three that were originally built on the campus, apparently dating back to the time ,when the cave man had still roamed the earth. The other two houses contained the Plant Operations office and the other, a battered woman's shelter, for which no one was to know about, for security reasons. Even though, as I had later found out that several angry ex- husbands and boyfriends would show up after the midnight hour on the first shift.

Jackie welcomed me at the counter, as her office was in the area that used to be the living room area of the house. She took my application, looked at ot and then told me that I needed to take a typing test. I thought to myself, "a typing test'? I could barely type the hunt and peck, two finger method. Mavis Beacon was not popular with the office staff just yet.

She hands me a memorandum about a child care conference and tells me to type it. What a relief! This typing test was going to be a breeze! This was not a timed test, like the tests you got in high school and teachers gave you nightmares about. I typed the memo, fairly well, I thought. Then she took it and the application and escorted me into the impressive office (formerly the master bedroom suite) of the Director of the Office of Campus Safety and Security.

I was introduced to John Becker. A very strict man who had previously been a retired Chicago police-detective-sergeant who was hired by the Director of Plant Operations for this job. This man was absolutely bald and quite huge in proportions to the others in the office. This guy did eventually hire me and I was on my way to finally begin a gainfully employed teenager and college student.

My hours were to be just two days a week. Friday nights from 4:00 to 11:00 p.m. and Saturdays from 8:00 am to 4:00 pm. My training, was to be from 4:00 to 11:00 p.m. in the evening on the Wednesday and Thursday, prior to my starting that Friday evening. I was to be trained by a Ms. Mary Doyle. Mary was a sweet person, at first glance, but that only lead you to a false sense of security. A housewife and mother,

I thought, married to some guy named Romney. She proceeded to tell me, droning continuously, over and over, all that she ever knew about being a clerk and dispatcher, to the various public safety officers, all around the campus. This was fine, except for one thing. She began her life as an Admissions and Registration Clerk. Now how can I accept this? Because she really didn't know the difference between a 10-28 and a political science course. This was a really terrific introduction to the cast of characters, whom I would come to know and then they would mysteriously get fired, quit or disappear. You see, the office was structured like a pseudo police department ,which it was to become some twenty years later.

At the nerve center of this chain of command (with emphasis on nerve) was the Director John, who wrote the campus book, when it came to safety and security regulations on what students and staff, you and others, could do and not do within the office.

The next level changes to something called Watch Coordinators (now Sergeants) to anyone else. One each for the three shifts that encompassed the twenty four hour period. One each, for every hour that the office was open. This remained a seven day a week service.

The cast included Bob Tuchfarber, on the third shift. Ron Visconte, on the second shiift and Samuel Mulle, the first shift man. Between these fools, I was placed on Bob Tuchfarber's shift that I remember so well. I hadn't been there all of two days and I had my first run in with Bob over the fact that, I had to answer the call of nature during my shift and didn't answer his call on the two way radio in the office for two minutes. My god! I thought that this guy had some nerve! He had a radio attached to his pocket. My radio was attached to the wall and I could not have the pleasure of having the radio in the restroom with me and still be able to answer this mans request. But I must digress, I realize now that it was a breach of security, but nobody told me, especially that I could not go to the restroom when I needed too. But he could.

My shift on Saturdays was sometimes under the direction of the first shift man, Samuel Mulle. The others on this same shift, gave this guy the nickname of mule boy, because of slight resemblance to a jack ass. This guy , who had apparently had no experience whatsoever, when it came to supervisory skills, people skills or public service skills at all. The only skill that this guy did have was that of barking orders, either in person or over the radio.

If you were on your thirty minute break and you returned to the office, one minute past thirty, forget it soldier! Your late!! This will be documented and entered into your permanent record! I thought, "What permanent record?" I was only a student worker here.

Well, four years later, I found out otherwise, that a personal dossier on everyone in the office was being kept my the Director and they all had some very incriminating things in them. This guy needed a huge needle to lance that great big fat head that he had grown. He was so full of himself that, by the end of my third year, he was finally fired. For what I don't know. Maybe it was in his dossier?

The last coordinator, Ron Visconte was a really nice person. Very easy to get along with. But, he too, was full of quirks and boy, did people have questions. He was of Italian descent and when he wasn't working for the college, he was a part time police officer for the Pinhook Illinois Police department.

What led to the many questions, was that you always stereotyped many Italians in movies and media as related to the mob and organized crime. Right! Well, about this time a very famous Chicago crime boss, one Michael "Big Mac" Salerno had died. Not by a drive by shooting or as a result of a rival gang mob hit contract or anything, just from a simple heart attack. Well, in the newspaper obituary account of this guy's criminal past and present, was his family tree, which happened to mention the Visconte family. Apparently when asked this question about his relatives, he would openly admit that "Big Mac" was his uncle, but that was a far as it would go. Nothing more, nothing less. You didn't ask and he doesn't tell. Don't ask, don't tell! Sounds familiar? Besides it gives one the uneasy feeling that you may be in the presence of a future crime boss.

In this pseudo-police department were two different styles of officers. Beat cops and motor cops. Some of the more memorable times on the job was when I worked the same shifts with some of them.

Jim Westin, a rather young kid at best, who was one of the motor cops at the campus. He spent the good part of his Monday through Friday shifts, riding around in the Safety and Security truck, complete with the red and blue bat light on top of it giving motorist assistance. Unlocking and locking doors on the campus and helping to unlock cars, where the owners locked their keys within, were his only duties. It seemed that this guy's whole universe was centered around cars.

I don't know, but I thought it was a macho thing with this kid. The kid was barely twenty one years old. This kid would always talk to me, when he would stop in the office on his break and tell me about his many aspirations in life and what he was proposing to do with it in the end. The reason said it may be a macho thing , was that one day, just out of the blue, he came in to talk to me in the office and started opening up about all the secret dreams that he had been having. Reoccurring dreams, about being on the job and providing motorist assistance to stranded motorists. The location of these dreams were always the same, somewhere on the hoods of the motorists vehicles and with the equipment that only he could provide. And in the dreams, his motorists were always satisfied with the service that he provided.

The other motor officer worth noting was Dawn Wolfe. Dawn was quite the example of a very friendly woman who was single, in her late twenties and very, very unusual. Dawn was the product of the late 60's and early 70's eras. She lived with her sister in the neighboring town of Minook. Her sister was an emergency room nurse at one of the local hospitals. Dawn was the type of person who would try anything just once in her life and try she did.

She dated various cocaine and crack drug users, including trying some of the various elements. Experimentation, apparently was the order of the day and try, she did. After drugs, she tried various different faiths and religions, as some are classified now. The most famous of these, was the time that she tried Devil Worhip, including such things like pentagrams, sorcery and vivid explanations on the numbers 666 and their relationship to Universal product Codes which are found on everything these days.

She even went so far, as to learn how to fly at one time. No, not without an airplane, due to the use of the drugs, but actual flying lessons. She tried and she succeeded to get herself, into the air, but only to fail again, by not having enough money to finish the lessons which caused her to moonlight at the airfield, washing planes to try and pay off her latest infatuation.

She was quite the unusual girl. When she was on the job at the college, she had this very unfortunate issue of not knowing how to spell correctly. Pity, for she usually succeeded in the other strengths that she had. The one time, she was on patrol in the various parking facilities when she proceeded to write various parking ticket warnings to various students. She wrote on the ticket in particular, which I had happened to find, when I was recording them in the official records, had on the bottom of it, the following message...NEXT TIME, YOU WILL BE TICKED! Not ticketed, like it should have been. After this, she became the brunt of office gossip. The difference between her message and a ticket from the local police was about thirty dollars at that time. Now it is at least $250.00.

In another instance, she had a very hard time, understanding and using police codes, which are the language of communication between the officers and the dispatchers. When you communicated within this office, you either used plain English or a series of ten codes. Ten one, ten two, ten nine, etc. Well, every time that she would pull someone over or stop to direct traffic at an intersection, she would promptly announce over the radio that she was 'going down on traffic'. Well, given the fact that she was the only female officer that worked in that office and given the male demeanor constantly misconstrued that she was stopping traffic to perform outrageous acts on them, like a cheap person of the streets.

This same thing goes on daily in a town about twenty miles east of me now. Every morning on my way to work, I see the cars lined up for the various girls, who are out there stopping traffic and taking Mastercard and Visa.

Having been employed by the college, now for five and a half years , I have seen many persons come and go within this department. It was never more apparent with the number of Director's that managed the office within that time span. I have put up with (yes that's right!) put up with at least seven of them. All of their little idiosyncrasies, their petty problems and their martial problems.

I mentioned out very first Director, John, who was a former Chicago cop, detective-sergeant. His attributes ranged from his running the office like a pseudo police department and he was the desk sergeant and intimidation was the order of rule. I wonder if he knew a John Burge. You didn't question his authority, because you really didn't know what type of wrath could be brought down upon you.

After a year or so, this guy started being nice to people, which was totally out of character for this guy. So I did some checking and Jackie, the office clerk said that he was just apprised of the fact that he had a new boss to report to and could possible be kicked out of his directorship before he could blink.

I thought that it was truly – about time that this happened. What a relief! And it did come to fruition, for within the two weeks of newfound niceness, he send everybody a memo stating that he would be accepting a teaching position at the college and was stepping down from his throne of power, effective immediately. This led to a point in the office leadership life, which ran the gambit of a total of six new Director's ,who would succeed him, in various shapes, forms, and styles of dictatorships.

The new Director, who succeeded John, was coincidentally named John as well. John Weiman, a sixty four, going on eighty, looking man, who had been with the department as an officer for a number of years before my arrival there. John, who we thought, was the grandfatherly and with good reason, that he was type. If you needed time off or to put in for vacation, there was never any trouble as there used to be, with the other John. With the old John, every time I wanted to take a day off or put in a vacation request, I always had to lie through my teeth. My cousin Susan, who lives in California now, I would always say that I was going to visit. For one reason or another. My reasons ran the gambit from her getting engaged to getting married, to the birth of their first child, to her being near death from a car accident on the I-5 to finally, after four years, beginning divorce proceedings against her, supposed new husband. Boy, what yarns! All this and my cousin is still single, dating and has not married. Yes, I probably would have been struck down by lightening, for all of this, if it had not been for the constant change of management in this office.

Enter the reign of Harry Foster, the third in the line of the Director's. This time, the office had suffered through, what we preferred to call CAMPUS GATE, something like WaterGate, but ten times more vicious. Harry too, was a part-time patrol officer from within the ranks. In his off hours, he was a full time fireman, paramedic, second lieutenant at the local fire department. Harry was from the type of eat, sleep and breathe fire department management school of directing.

Unfortunately thought, this guy had two rather major down falls, which eventually led to his demise as Director. He liked his booze, which was brought on by the stress of being a fireman and working for the college and the fact that he was having an extramarital affair with a lady firefighter at the department. Every time, you would see him, you would see them together, they were arm in arm, like a hood ornament on a car. He would often be in his office, quite late at night, after hours, with the door locked and you could hear them both, giggling, laughing and carrying on, in the throws of heated passion, when they thought that nobody else was around.

His final demise was the alleged report that he brought a gun to the campus and fired it off, while drinking alcohol from a brown paper bag like a whino. This was supposedly a set-up, on the part of other officers in the department that had tried to apply for the position of Director when it was originally published, however were not chosen. The rumor was that the Board of Trustees offered him a six figure income and the use of "business-woman" for a week. It makes you wonder what the state of higher education in this country is coming too and it still happens today.

The clincher to CAMPUS GATE was the phone call, I received from Mary and Jackie, that there was to be an emergency meeting of the office and we were all required to attend and that it was a boardroom level decision.

Arriving in the middle of the afternoon, I was told to go into the back classroom and have a seat. Everyone was there and nobody was talking, including the members of the Board of Trustees and the College President. It was like attending a funeral, except that the body in question wasn't dead, it was just sliding on a banana peel, sliding into a possible indictment for embezzlement and unlawful use of firearms on private property (this was before all this became felonies).

After the meeting got underway, it was revealed that Harry was gone as the Director and that the last person on this earth, would become the new acting Director. This was the last thing that I needed to hear, because this person was an officer as well, but was consistently trying to have me fired and wanted to bring in someone else, and I just would not go.

Before Harry, I should mention that there was one interim Director, Jeffrey B Webb. He was a watch coordinator on the midnight shift at the office and this was an actual recluse. This guy, no one knew much about. He lived by himself in one of the local apartment complexes nearby and nobody knew if he even had a girlfriend, lover, or was from an alternate lifestyle. This rumor was dispelled by the sudden announcement that this man was getting married. Who was the girl? No one knew anything, only that he was getting married and that from what the others surmised was that this woman had very wealthy parents and that it stank of criminal behavior and that maybe she was related to the mob. Who could figure? The other strange thing was that , he invited selected people from the office to the wedding and the week before the blessed event , he saw quite a few memos of regret that everybody that he had invited from the office could or would not show. Personally, I think he pissed off everybody for some reason, but that never could be substantiated.

The new acting Director of the department was Robert Padilla or as I preferred to call him, the Son of Satan and Evil Incarnate. Why you may asked was I making this judgment? Because that's was what he was, a snake with a mentality of Satan in the Garden of Paradise, tempting everybody, to do his bidding. Immediately, I felt the sting of his viperous bit, when out of the blue, my hours were cut back. I was working too many hours for my job classification, which was considered temporary, but that was not the point. This guy was working his evil from within the system to start a long road to get me fired or to quit.

Then it started. Jackie and Mary, the other office clerks started to pull rank on me, since they had permanent positions and I did not. If I inquired as to why, as I did not think I was any threat to them, all I got was the equivalent of "shut up and don't ask questions, you're in plenty of trouble as it is".

When I found this out, I immediately started looking for another position, preferably at the college amongst the permanent staff, which they had to offer. Unfortunately, he found out what I was up to and every chance I had at an interview, he suddenly had me scheduled to work, for no apparent reason, other than to infuriate me!

This went on and on, until I decided to apply outside the college to the National Rail Passenger Corporation. This was back when you applied to companies and they really and truly, checked your references and resume with a fine toothed comb, to be sure you were not lying. I went for the interview and was assured that the company would be checking my references and that I would be hearing back from them, one way or the other, in about a week to ten days.

A week to ten days passed and I had heard nothing. All of a sudden, one evening when I was scheduled to work and it so happened that Bob and I were in the office alone, he approached me in a very sarcastic tone and told me right out, that if I thought I was going to be able to get a job with this railroad company, I was clearly mistaken, And with that, he cut loose with a Satanic laugh, which led me to believe that how in the hell, since that was his address, did this guy know that I applied there, without my telling him, unless the company contacted him. Who knows? Who knew that I would get a second chance at that same company some fifteen years later, but tis time, I personally declined the offer.

After some months, having left the college for green pastures, my wife and I stopped to use the restroom facilities at a local gas station and low and behold, who do you think we ran into there? Bob. It seems that he was eventually fired, not only from his Directorship, but from his original job as a security patrol officer. His new job was cleaning toilets in restroom facilities at gas stations. How fitting, I thought! This man comes from the bowels of the earth with his Satanic like demeanor and here he is, rising from the sewers with his toilet bowl cleaner. Who says, "What comes around, swirls around?"

Bob's reign as a self proclaimed pompous ass was short lived, when it was announced that a John Pakozdi was being appointed to the position of Coordinator of Security at the college. The college had gotten this bogus bright idea that, security with all its scandals and problems, should no longer be a separate office and should now, he part of the overall, Plant Operations department with the former Director (now Coordinator) reporting to the Vice President of Administrative Affairs anymore, but to the Director of Plant Operations or otherwise known to most of us at the college as the Janitorial Supervisor.

This was the beginning of the end, not only for me, but for the office, as this move signified that the office had finally went down the crapper and there really was a department for it. John was a nice guy, whose background was a local police patrolman on the force where the college resided. His only downfall was that he did not have an experience in knowing how to run and office. The only thing that this guy did have , was the ability to kiss administrative butt, when it came to the Board of Trustees and the Director of Plant Operations.

I was always left with the opinion that he really didn't know what was going on within that office. All this time Bob was able to keep his Directorship (now called an Assistant Coordinatorship), where he essentially pushed paperwork and other things. Well, I thought, things were really bad, but things were getting worse and Bob was stikll behind his campaign of terror to stick it to me and fire me. I finally told myself, that I had stomached enough and went to see John after working hours at one of his various off-hours projects that he owned, with his wife which was a little import shop in the town and I stopped off there to appeal to him, that I really don't want to be fired and that my job was on thin ice, because of Bob's harassment. He really listened to me that afternoon and assured me personally that I did not have to worry about my job, in the strictest of confidences. As long as he was coordinator, I would still be employed and I was not to worry about Bob, because he had definite plans for him. I said, thank you and that I really appreciated his time and effort for listening to me and then I left. Little did I know that Bob would see his own demise in the world of porcelain thrones.

The last coordinator that I ever saw, was that of Leslie Nelson. This guy was a dictator of sorts in the way he ran things. Julius Ceasar had nothing on this guy. This became the most prevalent, when I discovered that the backgrounds of all the past directors and coordinators, were non police to some extent, from the very beginning when the first bozo was fired. This guy was a cop. Plain and simple, with a very shady and crooked past. He was political, right from the start and he knew, how to kiss the Board of Trustees butt. This guy had been a Hartford, Illinois police officer, probably since the moment, he got out of his diapers. His management style was very similar to the first director, except for one item which stuck out above all else. This guy would not stand for anyone or anything that would stand up to him or get in his way and then proceeded to clean house. By cleaning house , he had everybody on pins and needles for weeks. He wasn't the least bit friendly toward anyone in the office, staff and clerical included, unless you were born and bred from police department parental units. This went for everybody. The other security people in the department, especially those.who were moonlighting from their various other police department jobs, found this guy to be an ever so "enjoyable breath of fresh air" in the office. To the rest of us, the air just plain stank.

The liitle people as we were thought of in the office were just delegated work assignments and that was that. If, we had questions, then they should be submitted in writing to him. He was never in the office long enough for anyone to ever get a hold of him. Partially, because he was also kissing the Boards butt and behind their backs planning a political campaign, that would eventually win him a seat as a city councilman on the Hartford Illinois city council.

My demise came, when he was leading a group of unknown persons through the office and an important call came in to the office from the college President. He said that he wished to speak with Mr. Nelson immediately! Well, as I had been taught from day one, when the President of the college calls, you listen and then jump. Sounds a lot like a television commercial for a famous brokerage house. I had to interrupt him to give him the call and I was reprimanded and degraded publically, in front of these people, like I had just interrupted Charles Manson, in the middle of a gangland murder spree.

I was instructed to never interrupt him again in the middle of what, he was doing, every again and under any circumstances. I shuddered, nodded apologetically and said "yes sir". Not long after this, I received a telephone call one afternoon. A very cryptic telephone call it was! It was from the Coordinator, who wanted to see me that afternoon in his office. Not having been my regular day to be working, I had thought that this was very strange and had a nagging feeling that this was not right. And my little voice was not wrong.

I came into the office and saw Jackie and inquired as to what was going on. Her facial expression was problematic looking and she just told me to have a seat and he would be with me shortly. He buzzed her on the intercom and I went in. He proceeded to tell me the words that I had dreaded to hear. I was no longer employed by the college and then came a list of accusations and charges. I was impertinent and would not follow the rules, so I was hereby fired. Meantime I could clean out my personal effects from the office and leave. Nevertheless, I was dumbstruck. This was only the second time in my life that I was ever fired from a job and with most people, its an experience that nobody wants to repeat, but with the rest of everything in life, it does happen.

Some of the other things that went on at the campus, could have curled your hair. Take for instance, that one Sunday afternoon, I was required to work, because the office had a policy, that if there were classes or special large functions going on, the office had to be staffed. Right. I get to the door and the place is locked up tighter than Fort Knox.

I started to pound on the door with my fist, because one, it's was way to cold to be standing out here in the middle of January, with no way to get ahold of anyone on the campus, much less the office, because the place and the switchboard is closed! Right Again! After pounding on the door for a while, the door finally opens from the inside to reveal the motor officer Howard Wolz, just then putting his shirt on. The guy just answered the door in his tee shirt and underwear. I walked further into the office to reveal that he was in the middle of a sexual liason with his girl friend and wasn't expecting me to be working.

This kind of thing went on all the time, not just with the personnel in the office, but with some of the other lesser administrators at the campus as well. It was rumored at that time that the college President's wife, had a thing for one of the "just barely turned twenty-one years of age" security officers in the department. The officer David, was his name, told me one afternoon that this woman had come on to him in the parking lot of the local supermarket off campus. Being that he was "off duty", he got quite shook up by the whole experience. By my understanding, he was not very lucky with the women in his life. Well, he took down her license plate number and asked me to run her plate through the state DMV. I did and I was quite amazed at what I found. The plate came back to a Kathy Rowe, the wife of the college President. I told David, when he came back to the office, during his break and his face turned ashen white with disbelief. From that point on, I still believe, he watched himself very closely when it came to doing his job correctly. Always having to look over your shoulder is a terrible thing!

The college was a regular Peyton Place of wanton sexual desire. From the office to administration, it was just as prevalent as ever. It was "rumored" that the Executive Dean of Arts was sleeping with a female member of the Board of Trustees. It was also rumored that the college President Jim Rowe was having a fling with his secretary Laura. This would explain why Kathy, his wife was looking for solace with David, the security officer. The most famous "love affair" of all time was going on at that time too.

The rumor that the Executive Dean and the female Board member was true. This love affair ended tragically, with the couple going out for drinks and a little "whatever" after a mid-summers board meeting and the very next day, all four major television network news reports were confirming the disappearance of the Board member. She was found later, dead in the trunk of her Cadillac Seville, that had been submerged in a rock quarry, several miles west of the campus. I won't go into too much detail, other than to say that the entire incident is the subject of another book and a made-for-television movie of the week (and a bad one at that, albeit now on streaming video), which only aired several years ago.

So it goes to prove that you probably or yet, have to be a little bit of an insecure person, in order to work in such a place such as this, but having been fired, gives you a new outlook on the inmates that are running the asylum.

IS SAYING "Thank You"
AN ACT OF KINDNESS?

These days in our fast paced and often impoverished and sometimes rude society, do you think that people should say thank you if they did you a good turn or your did them a good turn on some certain thing or occasion?

It seems that the more we progress throughout life, the shorter our answers have become. To each other, we barely speak in full sentences anymore. Teenagers of the time, now just grunt, snort or make animal noises holding out their hands expecting to be paid, but for what they want to be paid for is still a baffling mystery because we have to now interpret the noises and the grunts to discover what language they are speaking and what we must pay them for.

The California Valley Girl syndrome happened many years back and was quite popular for its time. Words like *Oh for sure* and *Just gag me with a spoon, why don't ya,* has become the benchmarks for what our common language is built on today. Who knew that the Valley street walkers of their day would now be the great grandmothers of the texters and the tweeters and the pinteresting people that have a need to post a note every waking hour of the day.

With the advent and the constant second and multiple comings of the IPhones and Android tablets and phone that have been invented, isn't it time that we started to speak to each other again, albeit over Skype or other two way visaphones that we only dreamed about in the past and only seen in Jetson cartoons on Saturday mornings, Can we begin a formal sentence without a hashtag or ending of one in an *lol*? As a society, we have been forced to migrate to new technology as it keeps evolving, but are we sometimes, all the better for it.

With the mini keyboards attached to cellular and mobile devices, our grandchildren will need glasses and have carpal tunnel issues by the time they are age ten. By that time, they all will still have handwriting that would suggest that they are still two and three years and have not practiced their cursive writing yet. Cursive? What's cursive? It certainly does not mean that you are cursing...*lol*.

It just means that you have no writing skills that one can read? Why? Because why write a note when you can text it, or tweet it out to a couple of million readers on whatever social media page you have become accustomed to or are a member of.

But I must get back to task. When we go out in public and the business people are 16 years of age and take your orders at drive through windows only to get the order wrong when you get to window number 2, then *Houston, We have a problem!* The new working class of the day cannot listen to spoken word, only electronic words and music over social media. But to them, as they hurry and throw my order out the window at warp speed and then slam the window door in my face, I say...

Schonen Dank
Me siento agradecido por el regalo
Dhanyavaaa
Hvala
Toda
Dziekuje

Haben Sie vielen Dank!
Estoy agradecido por el regalo
Bahut dhanyavaad
Toda raba
Ich danke Ihnen
Me has ayudado mucho
Shukriyac
Ani mode leche
Danke vielmels
Te agradeco el regalo
Bahut shukriyac

But when it comes down to it......thank you!

I Wondered Whatever Happened to Me?

Just days after my ordination to the permanent diaconate, my bishop, Bishop Hungler called and informed me that the diocese was assigning me to a nursing home ministry in Mount Airey, at Sunny Acres Home. I thought that this was great since my time in secular life was a very rough Damascus Road in going from working where I was basically told off on a daily basis with fear of retribution to one where I could just sit, listen, help and quietly – just talk to people without fear of ramifications and retributions of others.

As I turned the car into the parking lot, I glanced at the building in front of me – a very foreboding grey stone structure resembling granite you would use to make grave markers and cemetery headstones, two floors high and equally as long – roughly about three fourths of a mile in length. I parked my car and got out my vestments, stoles, and Pyx, I would need for the Communion Service I would be leading there later on. My feet trudged slowly up the stairs to the door as I kept trying to remind myself that I was here to help others on their personal life journeys and that this is what I truly wanted.

The Director of Nursing, Emma Christine met me at the main Nurses Station and welcomed me. She said that Bishop Hungler had called ahead and said that I would be arriving and that I was also the new facility Chaplain and that I would be holding Services in the Recreation Room on Wednesdays at 1:00 p.m. and that I would be making visits to several of the residents afterwards that I could fit into my time during the afternoon.

Emma escorted me down the hall to a rather large room with tables, checker sets and a dart board hanging on one side of the room with a small table in the front and a chair next to it. The table had a small white cloth spread over it.

As I looked around the room, I saw several elderly ladies sitting in the wheelchairs with their attendants nearby and one gentleman sitting off to the side with an attendant standing near the door in the back. Very quietly I vested in the back of the room and prayed quietly to myself for God to make me and instrument of His peace and the wisdom to know the difference.

As I walked forward to the front of the room, I began with a smile and greeting my new lowly congregation with *"The grace of the Lord Jesus Christ, the love of God and the communion of the Holy Spirit be with you all."* Normally, this is where the congregation answers back "And with your spirit", but they all just sat there and smiled at me. I continued with the liturgy asking that we confess our sins in the presence of God and of one another. As I read the prayer and pronounced the affirmation of grace, I opened my bulletin and read the shortest Gospel reading in history, but most appropriate, I thought, for this occasion – John 14:27. *"Jesus said, Peace I leave you, my peace I give you. I do not give to you as the world gives. Do not let your heart be troubled, and do not let them be offended."*

After I read the reading, I paused and continued with a brief comment. *"At some points in our lives, we may have done something, said something or thought something out of turn, for which we are sorry about, but we are all human and God loves us still even though we all make mistakes, because He knows...He knows we can sometimes do better and the circumstances that surround things. So let us not be afraid to lives our lived in faith and not in retribution, either towards us or towards others. Don't let your hearts be troubled and don't be afraid. Amen".*

I walked to the table, bowed and picked up the Pyx and began the Our Father. Concluding, I turned and faced the group and said, *"This is the Lamb of God, who takes away the sins of the world. Happy are we who are called to the supper of the Lamb"*, as I held up the Host. I paused and prayed silently the prayer for reverence to receive the sacrament and walked over and communed the ladies in the front row. When I went to the lone gentleman, he started to cry uncontrollably, but accepted the Host from me. He said, *"Thank you"*, and asked if he could talk to me. I said *"Yes, but later on"*, and went back to the front and closed the pyx and said final prayer and blessing and dismissed the group with the words *"Be at peace, Christ is with you"*, and walked to the back of the room to take off my vestments. The attendants came forward and were wheeling the ladies out. Some of them thanked me by reaching out their withered hands and said "God bless you too Pastor". When I looked over, the gentleman was already gone.

Later that afternoon, I visited with several of the ladies who came to the Service and a few others. Then I came to Room 349. As I opened the door, sitting in the recliner next to the bed was the gentleman from before. *"Come in, Pastor, sit down"*. I replied, *"Hello"* in a startled voice. *"And you are?..*I continued.

"And you are?...", I continued. *"You can call me Ray – Ray Martin...having been at your Service brought back a whole lot of memories and thoughts about people, I've had – good and bad – for a long time. Do you have time to listen to a very bitter, remorseful old man?"* I said, *"I'd be honored"*.

He told me that he had only recently come to the facility after the death of his wife of 40 years, Anne, whom he loved dearly. They had no children together but explained to me that was what lead the both of them to many years in the education field, most recently as a substitute high school teacher. His wife was working at another school until the state declared an educational funding crisis and eventually …just about everyone, no matter how long you were with the district were rifted. Rifted being a very polite way of saying "your fired" but we will have you back if another position opens and you are lucky enough to be considered for it. This was seven years ago and up until she passed, his wife was getting less than $100.00 a week in unemployment and because she was a larger woman and after having surgery needed to walk with 2 canes, it made it unbearable on him that no one would hire her again, nor would that school district hire her back either. He told me that the Director of Human Resources from there quit right after they fired her and the others only to reappear as the new Principal at the school where he was working. The reasons at the time were unclear to him, but as a lot of events that happened after that "sudden arrival" eventually started to speak volumes.

He went on to say that this person turned a blind eye to a racial bullying incident of an Arab-American student getting the crap beat out of his in a bathroom by students, many of whom where on the school athletic teams. That incident was quickly handled placing the "person" on administrative leave and offering to settle the issue out of court. Shortly after, it was announced that the person "resigned" and left for another position elsewhere with their dignity intact.

Meantime, in a rare political move, the School Board promoted to Principal, the Athletic Director who, by no coincidence was a former student. The new Principal claimed he could do a better job than his predecessor and got lucky. He also was as crooked as crooked gets. One, he had no background other than his college degree, nor experience in running or operating a high school. Two, he had to know everything about everybody (coaches included), whom he needed the requisite political clout to get his position grounded effectively.

"It was once said that he wanted to help 'mentor' certain female coaches. Some responded in kind and sold their souls to the Devil, which is what he was. A few had respect enough to resign all their posts and then get out of the building, if they could afford to do so. For those that remained, it was like they sold their souls to Satan and became his personal eyes and ears. That was just the beginning.

One day, I was assigned to the library and was instructed to set up the library for an 'afterschool' meeting of his 'student advisory board'. This mysterious board met with him once a month but an a strangely

*odd hour, almost 45 minutes to one hour after school
had finished for the day. I waited until most of its
members arrived for the first meeting and then left
for the day, trying not to think about what went on
just moments before."* It was this grouping of what
he called "Satan's Minions" that joined with his adult
counterparts to eventually force anyone who did not
submit to his bidding into a very subtle bullying that
became more prevalent as it went along for those
employees who would not compromise their work
ethics, so that he could then fire them "at will" or for
no real reason and legally get away with it.

He said that as time went on, he had only a 30
minute break for lunch. If a teacher had a plan
period even if it was on the other end of the building,
he was "ordered" to fill in that hour and then return
back to the original room, even if it was back on the
other end of the building – and that building was
almost a half a mile long and with 3,200 students in the
hallways, you had a better chance of getting to your
destination if you were in a car on the expressway
at 7:30 in the morning. This went on for two years.
Then since he would not resign peaceably, one
morning he was in class and overheard the students
making wild claims to each other that he was an
openly gay man and that they heard it from one of
the coaches. Boy was this getting bad and making
for a very hostile workplace. In addition to this, the
Principal very quietly changed the "no electronic
devices" policy and allowed students to carry their
Smartphones, I-Pads, I-Phones, laptops, tablets and
anything else that you can instant message with to
class. He even allowed some teachers to allow it
at their "discretion". But some teachers that were

backing him and allowing usage for virtually anything and everything and others did not, but would not be clear enough to say that in their lesson plans.

So you could be in a room giving a major test and the students would be using their devices, very heavily disguised with their hands in their pockets, puling it out, in their purses, under their desks, positioned between their legs as well. When you would explain this to the teachers, you would get chastised, because you were expected to "ignor" the problem and only because this particular teacher or teachers were members of his community.

This went further one day when he came to work early and was assigned to be in the Metallurgy Lab that day. It was quite peaceful as he walked down to the Lab which happened to be located across the hallway from the Automotive Lab. As he opened the door, he heard wild school girl giggling and laughing in sounds of screams of ecstasy and then, out of the Auto lab door flew the instructor's service manager. He called her Vibranne. Vibranne was all red faced and out of breath, with her clothes all beshoveled, stopping briefly in horror that she was "discovered" and then running down the hall to the restroom. He went immediately into the Metals Lab and slammed the door. It was rumored that the Auto Instructor was a ladies man who was in the service and preferred to pull into as many ports of call as he wanted. His Service Manager was also a Special Education teacher in the building where they both had worked,

Sometime back, he was rumored to have spent time with another female substitute teacher, for whom Ray said, *"the students referred to as 96, because she moved about as slow as a 96 year old."* But she had no money and a car that hardly moved and she thought that, maybe, by offering herself in trade, she would get her car fixed. Well, he apparently didn't like a "tease" and got what he wanted and then billed her for the car repairs anyway. She eventually was fired, probably for not paying the bill to the district.

But the bullying, spying and snitching on everyone and everybody continued to the point where there was fighting amongst themselves and the building broke off into two factions. "Since the state, no longer acknowledges, nor backs any type of union in this state, teachers are still required to pay full union dues and for what? Probably to line the coffers of the heavy pockets of the political machines that dominate education today.

He said that he saw more teachers, selling their very souls to keep their jobs. "Students taking tests are all but non-existent. Students can now use their smartphones to post their student guides t various social media or just "twitter" it to about 35 or more of their best "friends", should they have the same teacher for whatever subject it might happen to be."

He even heard that Thelma Danforth (of the famous Reproducing Room) even copied tests (which are supposed to be secured) for her own children's benefit. She was not sanctioned, nor fired, but instead was given additional duties as an "permanent substitute" and still probably will be working there until she passes from this life over her machine or Adolpho, whoever died first.

But Ray's downfall came when he was to fill in for a business teacher, who would sell her own mother to keep her job, was going to a "female-only" business workshop and free lunch (or free-load, as he stated) presentation at a nearby banquet hall. This teacher always scheduled her field trips on the days when she had her worst classes, *"and I mean her worst classes"* Ray said. *"Those who could not handle any other classes and probably were still failing her own, which they were."*

But his downfall was when he was scheduled to give a lunch hour class a test, which he always followed procedure and the lesson plan to the letter that the tests are sacred. No notes, no devices. "Okay, one other thing, they have to take first lunch today instead of second lunch, because of the test", the instructor said to him. The students (or so he thought) went to first lunch. They returned and he got class under control to take the exam. About five minutes into the test, a student on the far other side of the room takes out his device. He spotted him and took and empty desk and put him out in the hall to take the test. He obviously was tired of fighting the "every teacher has their own rules for devices-rules", and let the rest of the class continue with the exam. "Two minutes later another student walks in and proceeds to sit down and get loud and extremely disruptive. He approached the student, who obviously was late to class and knew everyone went to first lunch, but he wanted to play on the groups sympathy by getting a mass group of students to force (or bully) the issue of letting him sit where he wanted to sit in addition to the student choosing not to take the test, but would not be quiet either. So he moved a desk up front and the student started protesting that he was being discriminated (not by race) because he could not have his own way – a new but common form of bullying.

He had about enough and called the main office to send a security person to remove the student. This event happened when he attempted to call the main offices four different phone extensions until he found one that answered. After the arrival of the person, who removed the student, the class quieted down, but the whole experience left him very upset and angry.

"The end of the hour came and everyone left. In came the next group of students and a girl that walked in and promptly sat in the teachers chair at the teachers computer". She was an African American girl and appeared to him as though she were 8 1/2 to 9 months pregnant. "She didn't say a word." Having just finished with the class from hell, he turned to her and politely said, *"I'm sorry, please forgive me, are you okay....are you ...*(this is where he made a motion of "expectation")*?* The girl responded *"I'm not"*. He apologized right away for he had no idea of who this student was, as there was no documentation that she even belonged in the class in the first place. He said, *"Your very quiet"* *, he said as he paused and then continued to explain that his new sister in law was also a person of color and would " talk you ear off". "Could you take these papers to the main office"*, he asked. He handed her the papers and she walked out and never returned.

The rest of the last class went well or so he thought until he stopped in the office. The associate principal under Satan took me into his office and said that he wanted to warn me in advance, "the student you talked to is a special education student and a senior that has mental issues and thinks that everybody feels that she had a breast augmentation job and that her father is a holy terror."

He explained to him just what was said and what happened. It was left at that for the afternoon. Little did he know that the same student reported the same issue to her father for whom the associate principal stated is very "puritanical" and a university professor" and demanded that he be fired immediately. Since he had no other problems in the sixteen years he was there, he asked that he be re-assigned, but the Superintendent said "No-he's fired". This all happened within one hour after school had finished on Friday.

When he came back to school on Monday, he was held in the front office until the associate principal arrived for the day and then was told to come into his office and "close the door". He said that he felt that sinking feeling in the pit of his stomach and he was right. He was set up. First, by the teacher who left no documentation. Second, by the school who did not say or document who the student was or if there were issues involved that needed to be handled or addressed and by the administration who would not back up their employees. He was made to sign a statement of what was said and then told that his services are no longer required and that he would be receiving a copy by certified mail and then was told to leave.

And he did. All before school started that following Monday morning. As he was saying all this, he could not help but hold back the tears, because he hadn't done anything truly wrong, but the job he had been instructed to do the same way for years.

Was he wrong? I could not say because I wasn't there, he was, but I could offer him some comfort. Two things came to mind that afternoon that I spent with Ray. One was that great spiritual that I saw in this man's amazing grace. How sweet was the sound as he explained his life's up's and down's to me. He thought he was a lost soul but now realized God had found again time after time. He was told all his life that he was blind and knew nothing, because others claimed to know more than he did. But finally he saw the light and knew better.

The American master actress Carol Burnett began her career at the young age of 23 working towards her acting career. On her final show over CBS television many years ago, I am reminded of things that Ray said to me and what I can remember from my own struggles throughout life...

"I'm so glad we had this time together, just to have a laugh, sigh and walk down the halls,
It's 7:09 and just before you know it, comes the time I have to say...So Long!"

"Good Night!", I said to Ray as I departed his room and headed down the hall.

It's a whole new world, I see.

It's a whole new world for me.

I am the everyman.

I am ME.

ONE IS ME
(And the Walrus continues...)

The times go fast – the man did say – when dealing with many things,
Of persons, places and even things – it plays your heart like strings.
But as time goes forward, so must I – the man did say – as craziness and kirfluffledness about.

From those visible and invisible – virtual or not.
Broken abused, marriage shambles – the man did say – but is it really rambles?
Of course it is but to a point, let's start that forest of brambles,

Dictatorships and cruise ships, what do they have in common –
Those that own and roam for their own good and not everybody follows.
But relative visits of eher and Xerox machines that move like Aretha – the Voice just sat and listened.

When libraries were friendly and only cost pennies andwhat was a patron to do?
Just eat, chain link and stay caged but present – but not so sweet and scrubbed,
But those that hurt others – maybe mothers, but are you sure they haven't their young?

But party down,
Because of the politics that got those – their
standard of gold,
But the poor underneath, should have their day
and so, very rightly so.

But as all is quiet, the Voice credit out,
Let's ask for questions and answers no more,
And thus, as well, it went on and on
Until I remained but one,

...ONE IS ME